River Run To Texas

George Chaffee

OGDEN PUBLICATIONS INC.
Topeka, Kansas

Published by Ogden Publications
1503 SW 42nd St., Topeka, Kansas 66609

Editor-in-Chief: Donna Doyle
Editor: Bruce Beggs
Assistant to the Editor: Julie Anderson
Cover Illustration: Carolyn Lang
Cover Credits:
Map reproduced from the holdings of the
Texas State Library and Archives Commission,
Archives and Information Services Division,
Historical Map Collection No. 39

Riverboat scene courtesy of Delta Queen Steamboat Co. Inc.

ISBN 0-941678-60-1
First printing, March 1998
Printed and bound in the United States of America

For more information about Ogden Publications titles,
or to place an order, please call:
(Toll-free) 1-800-678-5779

Fireside Library

Other books by OGDEN PUBLICATIONS

These Lonesome Hills	Letha Boyer
Home in the Hills	Letha Boyer
Of These Contented Hills	Letha Boyer
The Talking Hills	Letha Boyer
Born Tall	Garnet Tien
The Turning Wheel	Garnet Tien
The Farm	LaNelle Dickinson Kearney
The Family	LaNelle Dickinson Kearney
Lizzy Ida's Luxury	Zoe Rexroad
Lizzy Ida's Tennessee Troubles	Zoe Rexroad
Lizzy Ida's Mail Order Grandma	Zoe Rexroad
Mandy to the Rescue	Zoe Rexroad
Carpenter's Cabin	Cleoral Lovell
Quest for the Shepherd's Son	Juanita Killough Urbach
Martin's Nest	Ellie Watson McMasters
Third Time for Charm	Mabel Killian
To Marry a Stranger	Glenda McRae
Pledges in the West	Glenda McRae
Sod Schoolhouse	Courtner King and Bonnie Bess Worline
Texas Wildflower	Debra Hall

River Run To Texas

Contents

Dedication

To Donna, who offered me the chance; to Virgil, who encouraged me along the way; to Veronica, for her help with Spanish translations; and to Judy, for her love and support during the past 31 years.

– George Chaffee

River Run
To Texas
Part I

Change in Course

*S*ean Darragh's face burned crimson. His ears felt like burning lumps of coal. He swallowed in disbelief, then heard himself ask a pair of one-word questions. "What? Why?"

"I don't know how to say it any clearer, Darragh. The bank no longer needs your services, and your employment is terminated immediately. Mr. Goodwin will see you to your desk where you will pack your personal effects. Then he will escort you to the door."

Pushing an envelope at Sean, Henry Fenwick said flatly, "Here are your final wages and the balance of your savings account, all in cash. Take it and leave."

Sean wished Fenwick was playing a joke, but the bank president possessed no sense of humor. This afternoon, his tone was serious, even menacing. The young man searched Fenwick's face, waiting for an explanation.

Sean had worked nearly four years for the Bank of Grantsville, in the upper Hudson Valley of New York. He began as an errand boy. He made clerk 14 months ago. Sean was always on time, always worked hard. He learned quickly, grasping bookkeeping concepts with ease. His honesty was unquestionable. His reviews were spotless. But as an afternoon sun cast long shadows across Fenwick's desk, there was no further explanation coming. He gave an irritated wave to security guard Sam Goodwin who

1

responded by placing a hand on Sean's shoulder and muttering softly, "C'mon, lad."

Sean clinched his fists. He was not one to walk away from a fight or ignore an injustice. Now he faced the greatest injustice of his life. Perhaps it was old Goodwin's gentle hand on his shoulder. Or maybe Sean Darragh's proud nature took over, figuring to ask for reasons might be seen as begging or pleading – something he considered reprehensible.

He squared his shoulders and held his head high as he stuffed the envelope in a coat pocket, turned and strode briskly from Fenwick's office. Goodwin dogged every step. The security guard ached to see his young friend treated this way. Goodwin was a longtime employee of the bank. He wasn't so much a guard. More of a doorman or porter. He dressed in a military-like uniform, but carried no weapon, save a nightstick which he had never used. As Sean reached his work space, Goodwin whispered, "You weren't sacked 'cause of your work, lad. Rumor is, it's a family matter."

His words were of little solace to Sean. From the day his parents had arranged the position at the bank, Sean thought his future would be secure. He would eventually become head teller, then someday, manager. He would find a young lady to court and wed. He would one day own his own bank. He would become one of Grantsville's leading citizens. Now those dreams were shattered, worthless.

As others in the office looked away, Sean placed his dictionary, pen, notebook, personal correspondence and spare collar in a pasteboard box. Then looking around the office one last time, he defiantly shook Goodwin's offered hand and walked silently into the fading sunlight. The world outside knew and cared nothing about Sean's crisis. Wagons rattled down the town's only stone-paved street. Merchants and shoppers alike bustled past as Sean began to walk slowly. He had no destination. He was still in shock. He found himself in a park near the Hudson River docks, on a bench, the remains of four years' work beside him. He tried to make sense of what had happened.

Sean Darragh was born in Ireland. He came to America in 1838 with his parents and older brother, Tyrus, when he was just 3 years old. His parents hoped for a better life in America. Sean's father was a skilled silversmith. Ty apprenticed under his father. A formal education was not possible, but both boys were diligently schooled at home by their mother.

Prevailing attitudes and prejudice toward the Irish seemed not to affect the Darraghs. The family was Protestant and of some means. Still, Grantsville was an old, established town. The Darraghs weren't singled out for discrimination, nor were they accepted as equals.

The lives of Sean's parents ended tragically when both were killed in the worst fire in Grantsville's history, a blaze in a theater that claimed eight souls. Ty decided to return to Ireland and urged Sean to go with him, but the younger brother refused, saying his future was at the bank. Now he wished he had returned to his homeland even though he had no memory of it. One thing was certain. He had no desire to remain in Grantsville. The town had betrayed him. He was alone, an orphan and now unemployed. All he wanted was out. But where could he go?

Sean was an avid reader and knew something of the American West. Irish immigrants had settled a colony in Texas. "Aha." For the first time in his life, he decided to act on intuition and impulse. "West. I'll head West and start a new life." Having so decided, he relaxed. He was regaining control.

Sean tucked his box under an arm and headed toward his room at a boardinghouse, but piano music lured him to the open door of a tavern. In the span of his 19 years, Sean had scarcely touched liquor. But this was occasion to toast a new beginning. He walked inside, not knowing his life was about to take a sudden, even uglier turn.

No sooner had Sean stepped up to the bar, he heard above the din, "Well, look who's here. It's the wee Irish boy. Lookin' for a job, potato digger?" Mike Fenwick, all 6-foot-2 and 220 pounds of him, swaggered toward Sean. Son of the bank president, Mike was a known bully and oaf. "Thanks for making room for me at the bank, Darragh."

Sean wheeled around. "For you?" he gasped.

"That's right, digger. For me. I'm taking your job. Pop says it's time I work at the bank."

Sean leveled his eyes at Mike. "You got what you wanted. Now leave me be."

"I didn't say I wanted it, stupid. It's what ol' Pop wants. Hey, now maybe you can work here, cleaning cuspidors!" Young Fenwick kicked a spittoon over Sean's shoe. Sean jumped aside and instinctively put up his fists. Despite standing only 5-foot-8 and weighing 140 pounds, Sean was not about to let Mike Fenwick take away his dignity, too. The piano abruptly fell silent. Chairs scraped the floor as bar patrons turned to watch the confrontation.

Just as quickly, a burly bartender reached under the bar and slapped a club in one palm. "If you two want to fight, take it outside."

Mike glared at young Sean. "Well, what's it to be, Irish scum?"

Sean picked up his hat and box, strode out the door and placed his belongings on the boardwalk. Mike staggered behind, giving Sean a shove that sent him sprawling. A couple of Fenwick's companions stepped outside to watch. As Sean gathered himself, Mike swung. Sean ducked and countered with a quick jab that landed squarely on Fenwick's nose. The punch only enraged the ruffian. He rushed at Sean, but the more agile combatant stepped aside and landed another blow to the back of young Fenwick's head. Mike fell over a stack of boxes at the mouth of an alley.

Change in Course

Sean moved toward him, landing two more shots to the head as Mike tried to recover from the first.

Sean thought the fight finished. Suddenly Mike rose and whipped out a pistol. He fired a shot before aiming, hitting nothing. Sean rushed him as Mike looked down at the pistol, bewildered. Sean tackled Mike, and the two fell and rolled through the alley, struggling for control of the pistol. There was a second shot, somewhat muffled. Mike gasped, then Sean felt his attacker's body go limp. Sean rolled away. Mike's face lay partly in the mud, eyes staring at nothing. "No!" Sean screamed silently. "No!"

Sean grabbed the pistol and ran back to the street. Some men emerged from the bar to investigate. *Best to leave the hat and box.* He turned and raced up the street, the weapon still dangling in one hand.

Reason said it was self-defense. Instinct said to run. Sean listened to instinct.

Current of Fear

G asping. Panting. Running up wooden steps three at a time. Young Sean Darragh reached the door of his room at Mrs. Ince's boardinghouse. Fumbling with the key. Bursting through the door. Rushing to the window facing the street he had just sprinted. No one followed ... yet.

Sean paused to catch his breath. He caught his reflection in an oval mirror. When this day began, he had checked that same mirror and found his black hair in place, collar and tie straight. But during the course of the day, he had been fired from his job as a bank clerk, fought with another man and then had killed that man in an alley. Now his face was flushed, his clothes a mess, his brown eyes wide with fear. The ivory-handled pistol Mike Fenwick, his assailant, had pulled on him was stuffed in the waist of his pants. He gingerly removed it and set it on a dresser below the mirror.

"Sean, are you all right?" It was the voice of his landlady, from the bottom of the stairs.

"Yes, Mrs. Ince. Sorry for the noise. I was in a bit of a rush," Sean answered through the closed door.

"Well then, supper's at seven o'clock," she said.

There would be no supper tonight. Several people had witnessed the fight. They would be looking for Sean. The constable was probably already at the scene. Sean had to leave, to run. Right away. He began throwing clothes on his bed. He swept up toiletries and dumped them on top of the clothes. He felt a flood of guilt as he added a small Bible to the stack.

Finally, the last item. He wrapped the pistol in a wool shirt, then pulled up the blanket and rolled up everything, leaving bare sheets on the bed. He tore an undershirt into strips and tied the ends. He used a belt to form a strap.

His money! Sean patted his coat and felt the envelope containing his final wages and savings. "Thank goodness I was paid in cash," he muttered. He pulled a month's rent from the envelope and left it on the dresser for Mrs. Ince. Tucking his belongings under his arm, he checked the window once more. Still nothing. This time Sean forced himself to walk quietly down the stairs. He slipped unnoticed out the door and into the cool evening air.

Bank president Henry Fenwick was in a foul mood. Once home, he went straight to his study and began stuffing tobacco in one of his pipes. For the sake of family, he had fired a good, hardworking clerk. His son, Michael, could learn the job, but would he?

Fenwick knew his son was lazy and had taken up with a rough crowd. He'll grow out of it, the elder Fenwick reasoned. Perhaps a job and responsibility would do it.

I would have been perfectly content if Michael had found work elsewhere, but despite what little looking he has done, he has landed no job.

Fenwick lit his pipe and puffed angrily. He had given his son specific instructions to be home by five o'clock. It was now 6:30, and Michael had not shown up yet. He picked up the day's mail and was shifting through it aimlessly when he heard an urgent knocking at the front door. The maid answered, then came to the study. "Mr. Fenwick," she said, "Constable Jenkins is at the door. He says it's urgent."

Current of Fear

Sean's first impulse was to run to one of Grantsville's two livery stables where he could buy a horse. No, he knew too little of horses. He instead headed back through the park and toward the river docks. Now the park was cloaked in darkness. Empty, ghostlike. Only a couple hours earlier, Sean had rested here and decided to leave Grantsville and start a new life out West, in Texas. "I never imagined leaving under these circumstances," he murmured to himself.

The Hudson River docks were Grantsville's gateway to the cities of New York and Albany. A slight cove along the shoreline created an area relatively free of currents, perfect for docking boats carrying furs to New York. The cove attracted trappers long before the American Revolution. It became a trading post that became Grantsville. This night, the docks were quiet. Sean spied a grizzled old man sitting on the edge of the docks, fishing.

"Sir, would you know if there will be any boats leaving for New York this evening?"

The old man turned and looked Sean up and down. He spat and answered, "No, sonny. No boats running from here. Try tomorrow morning."

Sean suppressed a wave of panic. "I need to leave *tonight*. Not even a barge?" He knew it was hopeless even as he asked. Then he spotted a skiff at the bottom of the pilings. "Sir, is that your boat there?" Sean asked, pointing down to the skiff.

The man looked down at it, rubbed his chin whiskers, looked up and down the dock and gave Sean a toothless grin. "Sure 'nuf, sonny. It be mine," he lied.

"Would you be willing to sell it to me?"

"Well now, I suppose I could, but that'd depend on the price."

"I'll give you $6 for it," Sean offered.

The man expected an offer half that. He nearly dropped his pole in the river, but managed to check his emotions. "I'll have to replace her, so I'd need seven."

"Done!" Sean exclaimed. He turned his back to the man and counted $7 from his envelope. There was a commotion in the park. Two torches. Perhaps six men. One carried a long firearm. Sean thrust the money in the old man's hands, tossed the bundle down to the skiff and scrambled in.

"She leaks a little," the man said. He noticed the men coming toward the docks. "Friends of your'n?" Sean didn't bother to answer but untied the skiff and furiously paddled her away from the pilings. Had they seen him?

The grizzled old man didn't feel any remorse about selling a boat that didn't belong to him, so he wasn't acting on guilt as he ambled toward the party of armed men. "No, I haven't seen a dark-haired young man dressed like a bank clerk." But as he talked, two men kept walking toward the docks.

"There he is!"

The others ran to the dock's edge. Sean had put about 150 feet between himself and the docks. One shot was fired. He heard a splat off his port bow.

"Darragh! Turn your boat round and return to the dock ... NOW!"

"Hold your fire," Sean yelled. "I'm coming back." But he was not. He moved the boat around slightly, hoping he was far enough into the river for the current to move him farther downstream. He pointed the bow toward the dock, but then slowly back-paddled. The group of deputies craned their necks, trying to see if he was coming back.

"Paddle harder, Darragh," the deputy ordered.

"Yes, sir." The distance was more like 175 feet. Sean saw he was still moving out into the river. So did the deputies.

"He's not returning," one cried.

"Open fire!" the leader bellowed. All six men began

shooting. Five fired pistols and the sixth an old musket. Sean could do nothing but swing the boat around and paddle harder. He flinched as he heard the zip and whine of lead about him. Murky water gulped the shots and gurgled. A portion of gunwale splintered in front of him. Sean stopped paddling and lay still, letting the current sweep him downstream. The fusillade stopped.

"I think we hit him," Sean heard one voice cry out. The voices faded. He was unhurt.

The lights of Grantsville dimmed in the distance, replaced by stars overhead. Sean lay in the skiff and gazed at the heavens as the river carried him toward New York. He fell into a fitful sleep. His slumber was deep enough he didn't notice a large paddle wheeler as it slowly overtook him. The increasing noise of water churning under the bow finally roused him from his slumber. By that time, the boat was only 20 feet away.

Sean had time only to pull his belongings to him and roll over the side of the skiff into the dark, swirling waters of the Hudson. The waters swallowed him, and the skiff broke apart under the bow and tumbled along the underside of the hull. The elegantly dressed passengers in the grand saloon of the palace steamer *Drake* never heard or felt a thing.

River Run To Texas

Aboard the *Drake*

Shh-whump ... Shh-whump ... Shh-whump.
As Sean Darragh slowly regained consciousness, his first awareness was of a constant, deep thumping noise. His head reeled, but he opened his eyes, grimaced and hoped they would focus.

"Whoa, son," a man's deep voice murmured. "Just lie still now. You near drowned last night and you've a nasty bump on the noggin, but you're gonna be all right."

Sean blinked his eyes a few times, and the image of a man hovering over him finally sharpened its focus. "Wha ... where am I?" he asked, his eyes glancing about and growing wider with concern. The thumping was no dream. It was the rhythmic pounding of a steam engine.

"You would be in the crew's quarters of the *Drake*. We're on the Hudson River, probably near Tarrytown 'bout now. We fished you out of the river last night. Do you remember how you came to be in the river?"

Sean was now fully conscious, aware of his circumstance as he was painfully aware of the throbbing in his head. The man by his cot peered at him suspiciously through wire-rimmed glasses. His elegant clothing was in sharp contrast to the stark cabin walls. He was the ship's doctor.

"Yes, sir. I was in a small boat, headed for New York. I was run down by a steamer."

"New York? That's a far piece for a small boat in a big river."

Sean didn't reply. After a brief silence, the man turned and said, "Well, Annie, you caught him. You want to keep him or throw him back in the river?"

Ann Sessions sat on the cabin's floor of wooden planks. Her legs were drawn up, her chin resting on her knees. Her long dress was pulled over her legs. Only a pair of dainty ankles was visible below several petticoats. Dark ringlets cascaded about her bright cheeks. She was, in a word, lovely. Her face reminded Sean of a Renaissance painting of cherubs with porcelain skin, bow-shaped mouths and rosy pink cheeks. She flashed a charming smile at the doc and said with a shrug of her shoulders, "I s'pose we can keep him. We might even get some work outta him. But let's not put him at the wheel. He hasn't shown much skill as a pilot."

Sean was both entranced and dumbfounded. Turning to the doctor, he asked, "What do you mean she caught me, sir?"

"If it were not for Miss Annie, you wouldn't be here, son," Doc answered.

"Caught you with a gaff," she winked. "I needed help pulling you aboard, but I spotted you in the river, hooked you and hollered for a couple of hands to hoist you in."

"I'm obliged," was all Sean could manage.

"What's your name, son?" Doc asked.

"Sean ... essy. Uh ... Patrick Shaunessy. I wasn't traveling the full length of the river in one trip. I stopped briefly in Coxville. I'm on my way to ... uh ... Virginia." Sean almost winced under the burden of each lie.

"Uh huh," Doc mumbled as he stood and moved to the cabin door. "Annie, I'd best let your papa know your catch will live. I expect we can drop him in New York."

"Thanks, Doc," Ann grinned. "I'll show him where we stowed his things and be right up."

Sean smiled weakly and started to sit up. Then he realized

were gone. Gathering the wool blanket about
ed around anxiously.

hes are in the engine room. We put 'em near the
ry," Ann explained, anticipating his question.
and Bible are here." As she stood and moved
s cot, Ann's eyes narrowed. "I doubt you
u certainly *did not* fool me."

e," Sean began.

k," Ann shot back. "Patrick Shaunessy is not
ir Bible, and Coxville is downstream of your
ident with us. This is my father's boat. I'm
responsible for bringing some hooligan
his passengers."

Sean started to speak, but Ann cut him off. "And another
thing – *only* Doc and Papa call me Annie. It's Ann to you.
Now, tell me who you are and why you carry a pistol."

Sean breathed a heavy sigh. A moment of silence. Finally,
it came out in a rush. "Miss Sessions, until yesterday, I was a
bank clerk. I was fired for no cause except to make room for
the son of the bank's president. His son picked a fight with
me. That's his gun, not mine."

"You took it from him?"

"Yes," Sean answered defiantly. "He had no more use
for it. Miss Sessions, you obviously saved my life. I'm no
hooligan, but even if I were, I would never repay your
actions with malice toward anyone on this vessel. I am
honest and a man of my word. Now, may I have my clothes
back?"

"Not from me," Ann grinned slightly. "I'll have a crew
member bring them to you, Mr. ... Darragh, is it? If you can
make yourself presentable in the next 30 minutes, you may
meet me in the dining room. It's aft on the main deck. Good
morning, sir."

Sean sat rubbing his throbbing temples. Never in his life
had he met someone like Ann. So strong. So beautiful.

Once his clothes arrived, he dressed quickly, anxious to eat but more anxious to see Miss Ann Sessions.

Several days passed. During that time, there was a funeral in Grantsville. *Drake*'s captain, Joseph Sessions, put Sean Darragh to work in the engine room, but Ann persuaded her father to utilize Sean's good looks, manners and friendly nature. He worked the return trip as a waiter and kitchen helper. Ann began teaching Sean the workings of a paddle steamer.

Once Henry Fenwick buried his son, his mood turned from sorrow to bitter anger. He was upset with the constable for Sean's escape. There was little Constable Jenkins could do, other than telegraph other law enforcement offices, but Fenwick demanded more. He heard of a new detective agency called Pinkerton and wired an inquiry. The answer walked into the Bank of Grantsville just three days after Fenwick's telegram.

Cleve Everline was a sinister-looking man. He was fair-skinned, but hairy, with wavy black hair, a thick mustache and muttonchops. His expressionless eyes moved about constantly, noting details for further study, as he waited outside Fenwick's office.

"Mr. Everline?" Fenwick said, offering his hand. "I appreciate your prompt response. Come inside, please."

Once inside, Fenwick reached across his desk with a sealed envelope. "Here is everything I could learn about Sean Darragh. You might also visit our constable, but he's not much help. Keeps offering excuses like jurisdictions and manpower."

Everline said nothing but ripped open the envelope and began looking through the papers. He mentally filed what he deemed important. Fenwick sighed. "Michael was my only son. I want Sean Darragh brought to justice. If you can't return him here, bring me proof of his death."

Everline looked up from his papers. He didn't care about Fenwick's loss, but nothing appealed to him more than a manhunt. Tracking down a man who escaped nearly two weeks ago would be a challenge, but there was no doubt Cleve Everline could do it.

"Make no doubt, I'll find Darragh," he said flatly. "When I do, I'll put him under arrest or in a coffin."

Fenwick forced a grin and warned, "I'll count on that."

Everline didn't return the smile. He stood quickly. "I'll find your man."

"How long will it take?"

"As long as it takes," Everline replied. "Our home office will provide reports weekly. Contact them if you need to get a message to me."

Neither man could have known that during the course of their brief conversation, their target had stood at the rail of *Drake's* main deck, watching his former home slide by as the graceful steamer glided down the Hudson.

Arrested

*P*inkerton detective Cleve Everline was dispassionate and thorough. Only two days after he was hired to track down Sean Darragh, the killer of Michael Fenwick, he had interviewed everyone who had witnessed the confrontation at the tavern. He talked with employees at the elder Fenwick's bank. He even spent time with Sean's landlady and the old fellow who sold him the boat used in the escape.

Harvey Jenkins, Grantsville's constable, gladly opened his files to Everline. "We almost caught him," Jenkins told Everline, hoping to impress the detective. "If my deputies could shoot, we'd have dropped him in the river. Could be they did hit him. We couldn't get a boat into the water quickly enough to retrieve his skiff."

Everline was impassive. "Tell me about the victim. Where was he shot?"

"In the alley," Jenkins answered.

"No, Constable. Where did the bullet strike?"

Jenkins felt the blood rush to his face. Everline intimidated him. "Fenwick was struck in the side, about six inches below the left armpit. The bullet went through his heart."

"Did you examine his clothing?"

"Well, I, uh, I looked it over, yes."

"Were there powder stains around the bullet hole in his jacket?"

Jenkins paused. "Well, not that I can recall, no."

The constable blotted his forehead with a handkerchief. Everline's questioning caused Jenkins to realize how shallow was his own investigation of the shooting. But he did have one piece of evidence to salvage some respect.

"I *do* have the bullet," Jenkins said proudly, reaching into his desk drawer. "Here it is."

Everline took the heavy lump of lead and examined it closely. "Doesn't look like it hit bone," he muttered, turning it over in his fingers. "Looks like .36 caliber. Witnesses say Darragh pulled Fenwick's gun from him and shot him with it. Did Fenwick have a .36-caliber weapon?"

"I dunno," Jenkins replied, suddenly feeling even more inadequate. "We, uh, we never found the weapon."

Everline rose to his feet and pocketed the bullet. "That's all. I'll contact you once a week to see if you've learned anything new regarding this case."

Jenkins started to say he didn't expect any new developments, but instead just mumbled "Good luck" to Everline's back as the detective walked out the door.

A full moon sent a shaft of sparkling light from the Hudson River shore right up to the hurricane deck of the *Drake* where Ann Sessions sat next to Sean Darragh. He breathed deeply, inhaling her fragrance. Sean felt good again. They had become close friends. He admired her spunk. She loved his gentle yet assured nature.

Sean had never felt this way about a woman. There had been a first kiss and a minor flirtation, but Sean was ambitious from an early age and girls were considered a distraction in his rush to get ahead. Sean's ambition was betrayed by the nepotism of his former employer; however, his two weeks' duty aboard the paddle wheeler and his new friendship with Annie caused him to rethink his obsessions. Sean took to riverboating with great enthusiasm. He was pleasant with the passengers. He got along with the crew. He was quickly gaining familiarity with the *Drake* and with river navigation. Ann was teaching him well.

"We might make a riverboat captain out of you yet," she teased as they watched the moonlight dance across the river.

"Perhaps," Sean smiled. "Riverboating appeals to me more than working as a clerk."

Ann returned the smile. "If you want, I'll see if Father will start you in pilot's training."

Sean didn't answer. The thought of plying the Hudson seemed out of the question. His mind raced back to the fateful night when he killed a man. How could it have happened? He thought hard. Did he have a hand on the gun? Yes. Did he feel it go off? No. Did he pull the trigger? He didn't know. But he did know this: Because he let himself be goaded into a fight, a man was dead. This awful truth brought a heavy, almost desperate sigh.

"What?" Ann asked. "Wouldn't you like to pilot a boat, maybe even become a captain?"

Sean looked into Ann's eyes, watching how they sparkled in the moonlight. "Ann, I can't stay here on the Hudson. I must press on to Texas. That's my goal."

"Texas? What's in Texas? Nothing, that's what. You have a wonderful opportunity here. Maybe you won't take to being a pilot, but you're smart, Sean. You can be anything you want on the river."

Anything but free, Sean thought. It would be only a matter of time before a Grantsville citizen would recognize him and turn him in. He often wanted to confess everything to Ann, but never could. He couldn't risk losing her friendship.

"Ann, it's just something I have to do. I don't want to leave you, but I've got to go. I can't stay here." Dare he ask her to go with him?

Ann's eyes searched Sean's face for answers. "But why? I don't understand. You said you like it here on the river. Why leave for something you've never seen?"

"Ann, there are some things I simply cannot explain. But when we dock in New York tomorrow afternoon, I must leave for Texas. I won't forget you. I'll write, if I'm able. And someday, I'll return."

The tears Ann felt coming could not be stopped. This, as much as anything, turned her hurt into anger. She bolted from her deck chair and wheeled around, glaring at Sean.

"Then go ahead. Go. See if I care."

She began running down the deck with Sean calling out for her. It was a sorrowful end to a beautiful night.

As the *Drake* steamed into New York harbor the following afternoon, Sean went through his duties, preparing for docking. He hadn't seen Ann all morning. Once the *Drake* was safely docked and the gangplank set, Sean was busy helping passengers with their bags. He made several trips back and forth along the gangplank until the last passengers were safely in the packet company's terminal. Now it was time for help with the cargo.

Sean walked along the main deck toward the cargo hatch when a tall, angular man stepped out and blocked his path.

"Sean Darragh?" The question was spoken as an accusation.

Startled, Sean uttered "Yes" without thinking.

The thin-lipped man snickered and pulled a gun. "You're under arrest for the murder of Michael Fenwick."

"By what authority?" Sean gulped.

"I am representing the Bank of Grantsville, and I'm deputized to take you back. Now place your hands on the rail."

There was nothing, absolutely nothing Sean could do. As he gripped the rail, Cleve Everline pulled out a pair of handcuffs and moved beside Sean.

"You should've kept running," Everline said, almost sorry

the capture was so easy. "All it took was an examination of the captain's logs from several boats that work the Hudson."

Everline had just finished the sentence when a bale of woven materials hit him in the side with full force. He went sprawling over the rail, falling into the water below along with his pistol and handcuffs.

"Man overboard!" Ann called from where the bale began its swing. Grabbing Sean's shoulders, she cried in a whisper, "Run, Sean, please. I left something at your bunk. But just run, get out of here."

Sean touched Ann's cheek. So much he wanted to say and no time to say it. "I'll never forget you, Ann. Never."

Sean raced to his bunk, grabbed his rucksack and the envelope left by Ann. Then he sprinted across the gangplank and through the terminal, disappearing into the crowded streets of New York City.

River Run To Texas

Hello the *Woodwind*

Noble Sessions rubbed the stubble on his chin and read again a telegram from his brother, Joseph, in New York. Raindrops beat a steady tattoo on the windows of his Cincinnati home as his pale blue eyes scanned three terse sentences.

Sending good crew Sean Darragh [stop]
Should arrive by Oct [stop]
Is pursued by Cleve Everline of Pinkerton [stop]
                                            Joseph

Sessions laid the brown paper on his desk, relit his pipe, breathed a heavy sigh and watched the smoke curl from the bowl. So his brother wanted him to take a fugitive on as crew, he chuckled to himself. Why would he even consider hiring a wanted man? Why indeed.

As a riverboat captain, Noble Sessions was an enigma. Most men who navigated the Ohio, Missouri or Mississippi were somehow bigger than life. Successful pilots combined skill with bully bravado for profit and glory. None possessed more nautical skills than Sessions, but none was – or strived to be – as kind and humane as the 55-year-old captain. He sought only a fair profit and no glory.

Like his brother, Joseph, Noble Sessions was born to the river. He possessed integrity and a good heart. Not that he wasn't a good leader of men. He was. He was an imposing figure, a big, broad man with gray hair and muttonchops.

River Run To Texas

He had a gift of making his officers and crew feel they were the best on the river. He gave them a larger vision of their duties aboard ship. He was decisive and firm, but fair.

Despite these qualities, there was a high turnover on Sessions' vessel. This was due, in no small part, to his willingness to hire ... well, fugitives.

Yes, if this Sean Darragh fellow showed up in Cincinnati, he would be welcomed as a crewman aboard Sessions' 230-foot steamboat, *Woodwind*. Especially since he was recommended by Joseph Sessions.

It took Sean only five days longer than the telegram to reach Cincinnati. The way he arrived, however, was far more dramatic. It happened at the levee late at night as *Woodwind's* first mate walked the decks on his routine patrol. As he strode the main deck, a coarse whisper rasped through the night.

"Pssst. Hello the *Woodwind*."

The first mate wheeled around and peered over the rail. "Who's there?"

The response came from a figure huddled in a dugout canoe. "My name is Sean Darragh. I wish to see Captain Noble Sessions. I have a letter from his brother, Joseph, in New York. It was given to me as I left his employ."

"Come 'round to the landing plank, then."

"I'd rather not, sir. Would you take the letter to Captain Sessions? I'll remain here until you return."

Reaching for the letter, the first mate warned, "I'll put you in chains if you try to board before I return." Ten minutes later, he found Sean still clinging to the hull. "Come aboard, Mr. Darragh. Captain Sessions was expecting you. He'll see you in his quarters."

Moments later, Noble Sessions gave Sean a firm handshake as he ushered him into his cabin. "My brother recommends you highly," he began. "However, he sent a telegram that suggests you've run afoul of the law. I expect total honesty if you want work aboard the *Woodwind*, so tell me your story."

Sean explained how he came to kill a man in Grantsville on the Hudson, how he escaped and was pulled aboard Joseph Sessions' boat, the *Drake*. He described his near capture in New York and how Joseph's daughter, Ann, helped him escape once more.

"That's Annie," Noble Sessions chuckled. "I believe the man she knocked overboard was a Pinkerton agent named Cleve Everline."

"I didn't get his name, but somehow he traced me to the *Drake*," Sean replied. "If he's that relentless, I'm afraid he'll show up here. That's why I jumped from my train near Cincinnati and made my way upstream to the river where I found a canoe."

"Smart move," Sessions nodded. "A man came by yesterday, asking us if we'd seen you. I suspect he, and maybe even Everline, are watching my boat now."

Sean grimaced. "Captain Sessions, I'm already indebted to your brother and niece. I don't wish to bring you any trouble."

"Not to worry," he answered with a slight, knowing grin. "I've had some experience with the desperation and suffering of others."

Sean felt a rush of warmth and murmured, "Thank you, sir."

"We'll keep you out of sight until we shove off tomorrow morning," Sessions said. "I'll show you to your quarters."

Sean's *cabin* was a large wooden crate in *Woodwind's* cargo hold.

Sessions assured Sean, "It's only until we're safely under way tomorrow morning."

"Compared to a leaky canoe, it's first class," Sean laughed.

River Run To Texas

Cleve Everline lowered the telescope and rubbed his eyes. The first light of dawn revealed a blanket of mist shrouding the river and the dozen steamboats at the levee. It revealed nothing of interest to Everline. He handed the glass to his companion and muttered, "Still no sign of him."

Virgil Williams grunted. "The boat leaves at noon. A train arrives at 10. You want me to watch the station?"

"Yeah, but first we'll go pay the boat another visit. You stop by the sheriff's office at eight o'clock and bring him here. This time, I want to search the boat as best I can. If we don't find Darragh, then you will go watch the train station while I stay here."

At 8:30, Williams returned with the sheriff, and the trio went aboard and searched *Woodwind*. The search turned up nothing.

Everline's every instinct told him, fairly screamed at him, that this boat would take Darragh down the Ohio and Mississippi rivers.

He dismissed Williams and the sheriff. Then he went once more to Captain Sessions.

"I suppose I'll have to take my search downstream," Everline said. "How much for passage to New Orleans?"

"I'm sorry, Mr. Everline, but our accommodations are completely booked. You might try the *Pale Star* three boats downriver. She's leaving this afternoon."

"Very well then," Everline said. When they reached the landing plank, he turned around and faced the captain. "If you're hiding Darragh, I'll bring you to justice once I capture and deal with him."

Sessions was neither intimidated nor angry at Everline's threat. With no change in expression, he simply said, "Good day, Mr. Everline."

Thirty minutes later, the planks were hoisted. More smoke billowed from the twin 60-foot chimneys as the large side wheels started slapping water. With a shriek of its three-note whistle, *Woodwind* backed into the Ohio and turned west.

In the *Woodwind's* hold, a crewman freed Sean from his crate. "The coast is clear, Mr. Darragh."

"Thank you," Sean said, clutching the man's hand in both of his.

And, thanks once more to the Sessions family, his escape continued.

The Last Race

*N*ow ease the port wheel back to one-quarter," Noble Sessions ordered through the speaking tube. A hollow voice from the engine room confirmed the order back up to the pilothouse, and the *Woodwind's* port paddles slowed their rotations while the starboard wheel slowed to half speed. In the few moments, the 230-foot steamboat drifted gracefully and safely through a sharp bend in the Ohio River.

"That's how we do it out here," Sessions said to Sean Darragh. "If you carry too much speed through a bend, the current may help your boat to run away from you into shallow water. Piloting downstream demands more skill than plowing upriver."

Sean nodded. His experience aboard the *Drake* taught him the Hudson was a much wider and more forgiving river than this twisting ribbon of water.

"Did that maneuver cost us much speed?" he asked his captain.

"Only a little," Sessions smiled, aware of young Darragh's desire to put some distance between himself and the man chasing him. Then Sessions added, "Sometimes on the river, you have to slow down to win. That's a lesson some pilots never learn."

Woodwind continued to steam smoothly down the Ohio, smoke from her twin chimneys curling like a pair of corkscrews in the northern breeze. Sean had toured the boat from bow to stern and main deck to pilothouse, learning everything he could about her. Comparisons to his first boat, the *Drake*, were inevitable.

Woodwind was a young boat, built in Pittsburgh only five years earlier. *Drake* was more than twice that age, her launch dating back to 1842. *Drake* was a stern-wheeler; *Woodwind* had paddles on each side of the hull. There was a marked difference in crews as well. The *Drake* employed many black men as roustabouts and boiler room firemen. Sean noticed there were no Negroes aboard this boat, not even a chambermaid. *Curious*, he thought, but said nothing.

Of course, there was one other comparison: Both vessels were captained by the Sessions brothers, but the *Drake* included Joseph Sessions' daughter, Ann. Not a day had gone by that Sean didn't think about her.

Upriver, things were not so relaxed. Pinkerton detective Cleve Everline bought passage to New Orleans aboard the *Pale Star*. Then he gave her captain, Jasper Dumont, $50 and promised another $50 if he could catch *Woodwind*. That equaled a month's pay to the captain they called Monty.

The money was barely in his pocket before Monty stepped up the boarding of passengers. He even refused some cargo, not wanting to carry the extra weight. In fact, Everline barely had time to find a telegraph office to send this wire to Henry Fenwick at the Bank of Grantsville in New York:

Darragh alive and heading west [stop]
Anticipate capture soon [stop]

Everline

Pale Star churned away from Cincinnati a full hour ahead of its scheduled departure but two hours behind *Woodwind*. Monty knew Sessions. He knew how the careful captain would ease his boat downriver. Monty would fly downriver. If all went well, he would catch *Woodwind* by Memphis. Down in her boiler room, sweaty men shoveled coal into the glow of furnaces. Using all the steam her six boilers could furnish, *Pale Star* groaned and thrashed westward.

It was near sunset on the second day, after turning south on the Mississippi, when Noble Sessions turned his gaze from the pilothouse back upriver and first spotted smoke from *Pale Star's* chimneys, about three miles behind. Of course, he couldn't tell at that point it was Monty's steamer. He couldn't even see a boat. But instinct and reason made it a safe bet.

Sessions summoned Sean to the pilothouse and handed him a telescope.

"I'm pretty sure your detective friend is closing the gap on us," he opined as Sean peered through the glass. Sean turned with a look of concern.

"What would you have me do, sir?"

"*Pale Star* is a faster boat. But if we stoke the furnaces, we could stay at least 15 minutes ahead by the time we reach Memphis," Sessions answered. "I think your chances would be better if you jumped off there. You'll have more options ashore than pinned on the boat."

Sean nodded in agreement. "Thank you, Captain."

Sessions pulled the signal bell to the engine room and opened the cap of the speaking tube. "Mr. Dodgen," he barked, "there's a boat trying to overtake us, and I want to beat her to Memphis. I want full power from both engines and all the steam you can safely give me!"

Down below, a game of checkers was abandoned, and several men picked up their shovels to feed the furnaces. The pulse of *Woodwind's* engines beat faster. Engineers watched her gauges intently. Sean could feel the surge in power right up through the soles of his shoes. He packed his belongings, then returned to the pilothouse where he watched for snags or other craft.

Monty had spotted *Woodwind's* smoke as he paced *Pale Star's* hurricane deck. He also noticed the belch of smoke from her chimneys that signaled she was taking flight. Addressing the distant smoke, he said inwardly, "You can run, but you can't hide, Mr. Sessions." Then he ordered his furnaces stoked with lightwood, a knotty pine that burned hotter than any other fuel. Dark thunderclouds of smoke poured from *Pale Star's* chimneys. Glowing embers shot up into the evening sky. The race was on.

For two more days, *Woodwind* raced downriver with *Pale Star* in hot pursuit. Sessions' crew worked nonstop at the furnaces, but her engineers kept the boilers at safe levels. Aboard the *Pale Star*, caution was thrown to the wind as Monty demanded more and more speed. Memphis was only two hours away when Monty issued a bold order. He had a crewman fetch flatirons from the laundry. The irons were placed atop the escape valves of each boiler to increase the steam pressure.

From the pilothouse, Sean glanced uneasily back at *Pale Star*. She was plainly in sight now; she had cut Sessions' lead down to 20 minutes.

"I'm afraid she's just too fast for us," Sessions apologized to Sean. "You might consider jumping ship if we can round a bend and be out of her sight for a few minutes."

Sean pondered his chances. He was a good swimmer, but river currents were treacherous. He looked ahead and saw a spot about a half-mile ahead where he might jump and swim to safety. He looked back at the wake slicing off *Pale Star's* bow. Even with angry smoke pouring from her chimneys, Sean couldn't help but admire the boat. She was well proportioned, a pretty vessel with lots of gingerbread decorating her deckworks. He even smiled as he noticed a large star in the rigging of her chimney stacks. Then she was no more.

Sean saw the first blast, then heard its concussion as he witnessed with shock and horror a rapid succession of explosions. Each of *Pale Star's* six boilers detonated like a string of firecrackers. Her chimneys crumbled into an eruption of white smoke and steam. Boiler fragments shot upward like rockets, leaving twisted trails of smoke against a brilliant blue sky.

"God have mercy!" Sessions shouted. He jerked at the signal bell, and yelled into his tube, "Mr. Dodgen, hold off! I repeat! Hold off! All engines at full stop!"

Then Noble Sessions' voice was strangely soft, almost as though he had to speak the words in order to confirm what he had just witnessed.

"The boat astern, *Pale Star*, has just blown up."

Uncomfortable Words

One moment, Sean Darragh watched the *Pale Star* grow larger as she gained on the *Woodwind*. In the next moment – after rapid explosions wracked the boat – Sean witnessed a scene of utter chaos. Most of the deckworks were blown away. *Pale Star's* hull quickly sank and stuck in the silt at the bottom of the Mississippi. Debris was scattered everywhere.

Sean thought of his nemesis, Cleve Everline, the Pinkerton detective. Earlier, in his darkest and most private thoughts, he had wished Everline dead. Sean wanted only to start his life over in Texas, but under Everline's relentless pursuit, he was a hunted animal.

Yes, he had wished Everline dead and even imagined how he might kill his stalker.

Now, perhaps Sean's unspeakable wish had come true. This thought didn't please him. It had the exact opposite effect. Of course, Sean was not responsible if Everline perished in the explosion, but still he could not help but feel responsible ... and guilty.

The young fugitive clenched his fists and uttered an animal-like groan. "Captain Sessions, can we go back? Surely there will be some survivors."

Even as he asked the question, Noble Sessions was positioning *Woodwind* for a turn. It was a delicate maneuver. The *Woodwind* featured a pair of side wheels that straddled her hull. Usually, both wheels turned in unison, but now, as *Woodwind* slowed, Captain Sessions ordered the port wheel ahead at half speed and the starboard wheel reversed at half speed.

Woodwind responded quickly and literally spun around to face upriver in a dizzying turn. The spin brought shouts of appreciation from her passengers who had been summoned to the rails by the explosion.

A few moments later, Captain Sessions slowly eased *Woodwind* into the debris and ordered the launch of two rowboats to recover bodies and pick up survivors, if any. Passengers and crew aboard *Woodwind* prepared to take on and treat the injured. Space was cleared in the hold for those who didn't survive.

Sean captained one of the rowboats. He positioned himself at the bow and directed two other men who handled the oars.

"Make straightway for the boat," he ordered, pointing toward the remaining deckworks that jutted from the water. "Over there! Two people clinging to railing!"

As the rowboat pushed into the railing, the oarsmen helped Sean pull two women into the boat. Both were bruised, and one was burned from the scalding steam. They said nothing, but trembled and wept as they were rowed back to the *Woodwind*.

As Sean rowed out again, he saw several bodies. One crew wanted to collect them, but Sean said no. "We can't do anything for them right now," he said. "We must concentrate on survivors first."

Then he saw the head and shoulders of a man whose arms were draped over a piece of deckwork. "Over there!" he cried.

As the rowboat neared the man, he lost his grip on the flotsam and slipped beneath the surface. Without hesitation, Sean dove into the water.

Uncomfortable Words

In the murky depth, he bumped into a body and pulled it to the surface. The injured man gasped for breath. Coughing and swallowing water, Sean thrashed about to keep his rescue above water. The rowboat came quickly, and Sean held on until his crew could pull the man to safety.

Sean lay in the bottom of the boat trying to catch his breath. The crew began rowing for the *Woodwind* as Sean turned to comfort the man.

His legs were horribly broken. He wore only socks; the blast had blown him out of his shoes. The back of his head was so badly burned that no hair remained. Although his face was contorted in pain, Sean knew in an instant the man was Everline.

The detective blinked through the pain and water and recognized Sean.

Through puffy lips, Everline groaned two words: "Kill me."

At first, Sean said nothing as he worked to loosen Everline's collar, then he said firmly, "No. You're going to survive."

Everline felt for his pistol, but it was gone. He tried to grab Sean, but the stab of pain was so intense, his eyes rolled up in his head and he lost consciousness.

An orange sun dipped below the bluffs on the Arkansas shore, casting a fan of rays across the sky as the *Woodwind* reached Memphis. At her stern, the Stars and Stripes were flying upside down to alert those on shore to a shipboard emergency.

Earlier that day, three hours of searching turned up only seven survivors. A small barge steaming upriver had stopped and helped the search and rescue efforts. About 30 bodies were recovered.

River Run To Texas

The body of Jasper Dumont, the riverboat captain whose greed and secret pact with Everline caused the disaster, was never found.

As many as 175 people had perished in *Pale Star's* demise.

As the *Woodwind* began her approach to the Memphis levee, Sean worked near the bow, helping prepare the landing planks. The seven survivors were laid on stretchers and doors that had been removed for use as litters.

Once the boat was secured, Sean went to Everline. Due to the burns to the back of his head, Everline laid facedown on a stretcher.

"I'm sorry, Mr. Everline," was all Sean could think to say.

Everline tilted his head slightly to rest his cheek on the rough fabric.

He spoke slowly through the pain. "Why didn't you just let me drown?"

"I couldn't," Sean answered. "I'm not sure why, but I couldn't."

"You're a fool, Darragh, a gutless fool."

"Maybe so," Sean deferred. "I don't know. But I do know this, Mr. Everline. I am not a killer. I was only defending myself when Mike Fenwick pulled his gun. I didn't mean to shoot him. I'm not even sure I did."

Everline groaned weakly. "I don't care," he said. "I'm not your judge or jury. They're back in Grantsville."

"Just leave me be," Sean said evenly. "Give this up and tell your employer I'm dead. You can tell them I died in the explosion."

"Can't do it, Darragh. Can't do it. If I have to crawl, I'll track you down again and take you back to New York."

"Then you're the fool," Sean said as he stood up.

"Darragh?" Everline tried to raise his head and collapsed in agony.

"Yes?" Sean said as he turned to look back.

Everline struggled a moment, trying to arrange and speak

his words. For him, they were uncomfortable words even in the best of health. He didn't look at Sean, but stared into the dark fabric of his stretcher. "Thanks for saving me. I'll note your deed when I take you back."

Sean said nothing. He sighed, shook his head and picked up another stretcher to carry ashore.

Another Rescue

*O*ctober 12th, 1854
Abrd. the Woodwind

My Dear Miss Sessions:
We are steaming in good order for New Orleans and, failing any unforeseen difficulties, we should arrive upon the morrow. If problems arise, I cannot imagine they would be the fault of your uncle. His skill surely must be unequaled on this great and vast river. I have learned much in a short time and for that, I am deeply indebted to your uncle and father. Of course, my gratitude to you is all but inexpressible.

The man who tried to apprehend me in New York, Mr. Cleve Everline, almost caught up with us on the river, just north of Memphis, Tenn. Fate intervened once more as he was badly injured when the boat that carried him exploded. There was a great and tragic loss of life. The boat was completely destroyed. I doubt I will ever again witness such a sorrowful sight and pray such is the case. Mr. Everline was among only seven survivors we were able to rescue. He is receiving medical care in Memphis and should recover, but I cannot say how completely. He means to resume his pursuit of me if he is able.

Upon my arrival in New Orleans, I hope to find passage across the Gulf of Mexico to Texas. Please know that I recall with great affection and pleasure the time we spent together aboard the Drake and I hope one day that our paths might somehow cross once more.

Please give my regards to your father. I will now and forever remain

> *Yr. Obdt. Servt,*
> *Sean Darragh*

Sean pulled the paper near his face and blew gently to dry the ink. He folded the letter and stuffed it into an envelope with Ann's name on the front. Then he climbed to *Woodwind's* pilothouse and delivered it to Noble Sessions, who agreed to mail it from New Orleans.

"You're quite fond of my niece, aren't you?" Sessions teased.

"Yes, sir, I am indeed," Sean answered with a faint smile. "I only wish my circumstances were different. It would be selfish and irresponsible on my part and unfair to Ann if I were to act now upon my feelings for her."

Sessions' eyes never stopped scanning the Mississippi as he responded, "Circumstances have a way of changing, Sean, but Annie's a headstrong lass. It's good of you to be concerned for her well-being, but as you've already seen, she can take care of herself."

"Yes, sir," Sean smiled broadly. He remembered how Ann had saved him from the Hudson River, how she confronted him when he tried to lie about his identity, and how she saved him again by knocking Everline off her boat. "She can hold her own."

Sessions looked at Sean and grinned. Then he returned his gaze to the river. "Well then, my only advice is this: Should you wish to court Ann, don't wait too long, until you think you're established and your future is secure. Like I said, circumstances have a way of changing – sometimes for better, sometimes for worse."

Sean pondered Sessions' words for a moment. "If I find opportunity in Texas, if I see I have a chance to build a future there, I will return for Ann."

Another Rescue

Then, as an afterthought, he added, "If she will have me."

With her passengers standing at the rails and taking in the sights, *Woodwind* reached New Orleans at mid-morning. The levees were crowded with steamboats, barges and square-rigged schooners. The senior pilot deftly handled the wheel as the captain issued orders to the engine room while *Woodwind* eased between two other steamboats.

Using a megaphone, Sean relayed orders to the deckhands. Then, once the boat was safely docked, he helped the passengers unload. Remembering what had happened in New York, Sean kept an eye on the crowd ashore, searching for anyone who looked like they might be looking for him. This time, he found no one.

Sessions told Sean the *Woodwind* would be in New Orleans for four days and while she was there, Sean was welcome to sleep aboard while he looked for passage to Texas. And as his brother, Joseph, had done, Sessions wrote Sean a letter of recommendation to help in his search for a Texas-bound vessel.

It took Sean only two days to find work aboard a government sloop taking a survey crew to Boca del Rio, Texas. It was going to be deckhand duty, but Sean was grateful for the passage. He also reasoned this break with the Sessions family might help cover his tracks. The sloop wouldn't leave for a week, so Sean helped Sessions prepare the *Woodwind* for her next trip upriver to Cincinnati.

Some of *Woodwind's* passengers boarded the evening before her departure. As he helped the passengers find their cabins, Sean noticed several were traveling with Negro servants, butlers and maids.

The crew of the steamer also changed colors. On the downriver trip, the entire crew was white. Most of that crew left the boat in New Orleans, and most of the replacements were black. Sean watched in puzzlement as the regulars schooled the Negroes on the boat and their duties aboard her.

It was when Sean paid a final visit to the engine room on departure day that he learned the real mission of Noble Sessions and his boat. Sean was cleaning out his footlocker when he heard a voice from the engine room. It was the chief engineer, Daniel Dodgen, instructing a trio of black men on the operations of the furnaces, boilers and engine.

The room was hot and steamy. None of the new crew wore shirts, and the backs of two men bore several long and jagged scars. Sessions came up behind Sean, who looked over his shoulder and greeted his captain and mentor.

"What happened to them?" Sean asked.

"They are slaves," Sessions answered. "Or at least, they *were* slaves. Now they're working their way to freedom."

"And the chambermaids and servants?"

"The same. Sean, do you remember when you came aboard in Cincinnati and said you didn't want to bring me any trouble?" As Sean nodded, Sessions continued, "And remember how I answered? I said I was no stranger to the desperation and suffering of others. Well, this is what I meant."

At that moment, it all made sense to Sean. But he still asked the question. "Are you in the business of taking runaway slaves up North?"

"Yes, son, I am," Sessions confirmed. "But it's a business that pays nothing. Many of my passengers and crew are volunteers who help these people find freedom. I make money carrying cargo, but my real business is helping Negroes escape slavery."

Later, on the texas deck, Sean shook Noble Sessions' hand for the last time. As the two said their goodbyes, a well-dressed family boarded the *Woodwind*, accompanied

Another Rescue

by a Negro man and woman posing as servants.

The scene prompted one final question from Sean. "Captain Sessions, there must be thousands and thousands of slaves throughout the South. How can what you're doing possibly make any difference?"

"Look at their faces, Sean," Sessions smiled. "We've made a difference for those two."

Sean patted the shoulder of the man beside him and said in a soft voice, "Goodbye, Captain, and Godspeed." And with that, he picked up his belongings and walked down *Woodwind's* landing plank for the final time.

You'll Do For Texas

F all was coming to the Hudson Valley in New York. Leaves were just beginning their turn to the red and gold of autumn. There was even some frost the morning Cleve Everline limped across the Grantsville docks to begin his journey southwest.

It had been 11 months since Everline's legs were broken in a steamboat explosion. The Pinkerton detective had tried to capture Sean Darragh, the killer of a Grantsville banker's son. But the accident sent Everline first to a hospital in Memphis and then to New York. He had spent the last four months recuperating in Grantsville where he used his time to learn more about Darragh's crime.

Through letters, interviews, telegrams and a bit of luck, Everline learned his fugitive was in Texas. Once more, the persistent detective set off to catch up with Sean. This time, however, he had a partner.

"Good morning, Mr. Everline," the pretty young woman greeted at the landing plank of the steamboat *Drake*.

"Good morning, Miss Sessions," Everline answered, shifting his cane and tipping his hat. "Are you ready to help me track down Sean Darragh?"

"Yes, sir, I'm looking forward to it," Ann Sessions answered.

"Then let's get started."

River Run To Texas

It was three weeks later when Sean Darragh gave the wheel a slight turn to the right as he intentionally overshot the docks. Then he cut his engines and put his boat hard to port, allowing his speed and the river's current to sweep him back toward the piers. Just a touch of reverse engine brought the vessel to a neat landing at Matamoros, Mexico.

Sean had been on the Rio Grande River for nearly a year, first working for D. Latham & Co. as a bookkeeper. In his spare time, he did a lot of observing from the wheelhouse. Later, he substituted as a pilot on one of the company's three riverboats. Finally, he bought into the business and piloted the *James H. Dawkins*, a 200-ton stern-wheeler.

The 67-foot boat drew just over 2 feet of water and, on the Rio Grande, was nicknamed a "mud-skimmer."

Sean viewed the nickname with affection. He was in love with Texas, in love with his steamboat enterprise. His mud-skimmer carried cargo and some passengers from Boca del Rio, Texas, up the Rio Grande to Brownsville, Matamoros, and – if the river was up enough – all the way to Reynosa. Most trips were only a few hours each way.

It was hard to imagine Sean would take to Texas as he did, especially when one considered the circumstances in which he met one of his business partners, Dudley Latham.

The meeting happened in Brownsville, only four days after Sean arrived. His first order of business was to purchase a new suit and a holster for his gun, the Colt pocket pistol that once belonged to Mike Fenwick, the man whose death had launched Sean's year as a fugitive from unjust accusers.

Dressed in his new suit, Sean dropped in on a party of businessmen celebrating the arrival of Latham's new steamboat, the *Nuevo Sueno*. Food and drink were plentiful at the Elizabeth Street hotel. The mood was jovial. But when Sean introduced himself to the man everyone addressed as "Dud," the young businessman's eyes narrowed.

You'll Do For Texas

"Mr. Darragh," he said, "most men who come to Texas are lawmen or fugitives from the law. Which category are you in?"

Sean unbuttoned his suit coat in case he had to draw his gun. His eyes met Dud's challenge. "Mr. Latham, I would fall into the latter category. And which category best describes you, sir?"

Dud's face creased into a big grin, and he grabbed Sean's shoulder. "You'll do for Texas, Mr. Darragh. Let me get you a drink."

From that point, the two men became good friends, and Sean found a business and countryside that suited him perfectly. The opportunities Sean hoped to find in Texas were everywhere in the wild and untamed country.

The area between the Rio Grande and Nueces rivers was called Wild Horse Desert after the hundreds of wild mustangs that roamed through the brush. It was harsh, unforgiving country, but towns like Brownsville, Indianola and Corpus Christi were alive with commerce and growth.

"*Hola*, Señor Darragh," grinned the dock foreman at Matamoros. "*¿No tienes nada para mi?*"

"*Sí*," Sean smiled back, pointing to a dozen large crates. "*Tengo muchas cajas.*"

Four longshoremen quickly shuffled up the landing plank and began carrying crates to the dock. Sean's crew assisted in the unloading as he handled the paperwork.

The foreman, Miguel Sanchos, said little as Sean checked off the cargo. He spoke only a little English, and he knew Sean's Spanish was limited as well. As Sean looked up, Miguel asked, "Señor Darragh, you go to Reynosa today?"

"*Sí*, Miguel," Sean answered. "If the river is up enough."

"Then I have *tres* passengers for you."

"I must leave as soon as we load your *cajas*," Sean reminded. "Are your passengers here?"

"*Sí, un momento*," Miguel implored as he hurried away, off the boat and toward an office. In a minute, Miguel led two women and a boy of perhaps 14 toward the *James H. Dawkins*. The boy lugged a large chest, with some difficulty.

An elderly woman carried a small bag. She was stooped and stern, eyeing Sean with suspicion. She said nothing to Sean, but ordered the boy to place the chest on the deck.

The other woman was young, perhaps only 16 or 17. She wore a hat and veil and kept her head lowered, looking down at the deck as though she'd lost something.

"Señor Darragh, allow me to introduce Señora Yolanda Ellena Flores and," he gestured toward the young lady, "Señorita Catharine del Carmen." Pointing to the boy, he finished, "And this is Paco."

Sean tipped his hat and smiled at the trio. Paco grinned shyly; the señora grunted. The young woman looked up. Sean almost gasped. Her skin was dark, her hair raven, her lips full and her eyes ... they were so dark Sean saw his reflection in them. He felt himself staring as she nodded hello with a shy smile.

Sean quickly glanced away at her companion. Too late! Her eyes burned with a look that bordered on hatred, and she took Catharine's arm and steered her to a spot a few feet away. Longshoremen observed the introductions with snickers and muttered words that needed no translation. They loaded the last boxes and scurried down the landing plank, almost giggling as they went.

"The trip should take only six hours, seven at the most," Sean said. "They are welcome to my cabin on the texas deck. It catches the breeze and is the coolest. We should arrive before sunset."

To his surprise, it was Paco who translated for the women. Miguel led them up the stairs to Sean's cabin.

Sean blew a sigh that lasted several seconds. "Whoo boy!" was all Sean could say to himself. Then he shook his head, as if he was trying to shake her image from his mind.

Seeing a woman that beautiful only reminded him of Ann.

He climbed to the pilothouse and barked the orders to cast off for Reynosa.

Incident at Devil's Elbow

*T*he *James H. Dawkins* labored slowly up the Rio Grande, her paddle wheel thrashing evenly through the blue-green waters. Two crewmen tossed lines from the port and starboard sides of the bow, calling the depths back to Sean Darragh in the wheelhouse.

Reynosa was only 60 miles from Matamoros, but a drought had brought the river down. Now, only halfway there, Sean worried if he could make his destination.

"Can we get through, Señor Darragh?" It was Paco, the young Mexican servant to Catharine del Carmen and her aunt.

"We have this section and one more where the water is very shallow," Sean answered. "I'm not sure we can make it all the way."

"Señorita will not be disappointed if we must turn back," Paco advised. "She is on her way to meet her future husband. It is arranged."

Sean thought, *Lucky fella*, but asked instead, "So Señorita Del Carmen is not happy with her family's choice?"

"No," Paco answered quickly. "But this is just a visit to his family. Perhaps she will change her mind. Her family's rancho shares the same boundary with his rancho. I think her father and this man have agreed to the union so both ranchos may be joined one day."

Sean had one other question: "How did you learn to speak

English, Paco?"

"It was during our war with the United States. I was a servant in a Mexican unit captured in battle. I was in prison for nearly a year, and I learned English from the guards."

Catharine suddenly appeared behind the boy. *"Paco, ayúdame. Ahora."*

Paco shrugged and followed Catharine back to the captain's cabin.

Sean turned his thoughts back to the river, wondering if his boat could thread its way to Reynosa.

From a distant hill, a pair of brown eyes watched the *James H. Dawkins* steam slowly up the Rio Grande. A sombrero was pushed back on the observer's head. He held a telescope to one eye and drew a quick breath when he spotted Catharine's brief appearance on the upper deck.

His name was Eliseo Corantino Flores, but his friends had nicknamed him Cheo. Born to a wealthy family, he was bright and aggressive. He was to inherit the Santa Estefana, a huge expanse of land between the Rio Grande and the Nueces rivers in the area called Wild Horse Desert. It was a Spanish land grant to Cheo's family and covered 12 square leagues, about 53,000 acres.

Cheo ran some cattle on the property, but the family's base of operations was near Monterrey, Mexico. There was but one building on Santa Estefana, a deserted adobe hacienda.

Treaties that ended the Mexican-American War also surrendered the land to Texas and the United States. Cheo felt betrayed and turned his wrath on the gringo. He raided small ranches, scattered cattle and set grass fires to disrupt the settlement of what he felt was his land. In reality, it was, but Cheo was Mexican and wanted no part of owning property in the United States. Cheo had not attacked any boats on the Rio Grande, but that was about to change.

He scampered down from his rocky perch and took his horse's reins from one of two banditos. "*¡Anda! ¡Pronto!*" he cried as he led his two companions toward a bend in the river where he knew shallow water would halt the gringo captain and the *James H. Dawkins*.

About 40 miles upstream from Matamoros, the Rio Grande twists north, then quickly back to the west. The bend is known as Codo del Diablo, or Devil's Elbow. Cheo and his two companions arrived at a small bluff overlooking the bend just a few minutes before the *James H. Dawkins* steamed into view.

As Cheo predicted, Sean's boat scraped the river bottom and lurched to a stop. Sean groaned and ordered the engines reversed. The paddle wheel bit into the muddy waters, but the boat sat on the sandbar, not budging an inch. Sean added more steam and increased the wheel's speed. Still nothing.

"*¡Buenas tardes, amigos!*" Cheo called from the bank. "We can help!"

Even as Sean yelled back he could work the boat off the sandbar by himself, Cheo spurred his horse into the river and right up to the boat. The water came only to his mount's belly, and Cheo slipped from the saddle and over the rail like a cat, looping the reins around a cleat. The two horsemen with Cheo rode up beside his mount.

Sean saw Cheo approach and ordered a crewman to intercept him and turn him back. At the same time, Paco, Catharine and the old woman emerged from their cabin, curious about the grounding of the boat. The crewman met Cheo at the stairway between the texas and hurricane decks, out of sight from the wheelhouse. Cheo spoke in Spanish, smiling broadly and holding out his hands, palms up, to indicate he didn't understand the crewman's instructions.

The crewman tried to lead Cheo down the stairs when Cheo whipped out his gun and, with a sharp blow, clubbed the crewman unconscious. He grabbed the young man around the waist and cushioned his fall to avoid making noise. Then he holstered his pistol and bounded up the steps to the wheelhouse, the silver rowels of his spurs ringing like tiny cymbals.

"Señor," Cheo said, greeting Sean with a toothy smile. "My men and I will help get your boat off the sand."

"I *said* I didn't need any help," Sean growled. "Now *get off* my boat."

"No, no, Señor. You need us." Cheo never quit smiling. "We are happy to help."

Sean wasn't the only one who wanted the dashing young Mexican off the boat. Catharine's matron began yelling excitedly and trying to urge Catharine back into the cabin. Catharine resisted, and both women shuffled about the deck, about 20 feet from the wheelhouse. At the same time another crewman discovered the unconscious man on the stairs and called for help.

Sean turned toward the commotion behind him. It gave Cheo the opening he sought. In a single motion, his right hand reached across and jerked the firearm from his holster. He struck upward, the cylinder hitting the back of Sean's head. Stunned, Sean wheeled around. At the same instant, Cheo struck him squarely in the jaw with his left hand and Sean crumpled to his knees. One more blow with the pistol and an inky blackness swept over Sean. He sprawled facedown on the deck.

The women screamed. Chaos broke out everywhere. Cheo's banditos began firing their pistols, hitting no one, but keeping the crew at bay. Cheo walked calmly over to the women, grabbed Catharine's wrist and jerked her away from her screaming chaperone. He raised his pistol at Paco and glared, but said nothing. Paco stood motionless. Cheo led Catharine down the stairs and threw her onto his horse. He mounted behind her, grabbed the reins and spurred his horse away as his men backed toward their horses, firing an occasional shot.

A crewman pulled a rifle from a locker and rushed to a cabin door. Cheo was already out of sight, but the two horsemen behind him were only a hundred feet from the riverbank. The rifle barked a single shot, and one bandito slumped forward in his saddle. Both horsemen rode on and disappeared around the bluff.

Smoke continued to drift from the chimney of the *James H. Dawkins*. The paddle wheel continued its useless turns in the muddy water.

Except for the weeping of Catharine's chaperone, a strange silence fell over the boat.

An Unlikely Group of Rescuers

*E*ven before the pain, the first thing Sean Darragh felt as he regained consciousness was rage. He was angry for grounding his steamboat at Devil's Elbow. He was madder still because the banditos who kidnapped Catharine del Carmen were able to come aboard so easily. And Sean was furious he had turned away from Cheo, giving the Mexican outlaw the chance to club him with his gun.

Now Sean's head throbbed from two blows, one to the base of his neck and one to his crown. Cheo had used an old Walker Army pistol acquired during the war. Fifteen inches long, it weighed more than 4 pounds and was used as a club as often as a firearm. Sean was lucky to escape without a fractured skull, but he felt anything but lucky.

He blinked a few times and looked about him. Two crewmen, First Mate Robert Black and Steward Glen Koch, had rolled him over. Black used a damp towel to dab away the blood from a cut on Sean's head.

"Fill me in, Mr. Black," Sean groaned. "What happened?"

"They kidnapped the young lady. They didn't take anything else. Just put a few bullet holes in the woodwork. I think we wounded one of them as they rode off."

Sean rolled to his side and sat up on the deck, his head spinning. "All on horseback?"

"Yes, sir. They rode south on the Mexican side, around that bluff. The one who took the girl is riding double with her in the saddle."

Paco, Catharine's young servant, slipped between the two men. "Señor Darragh, I know where they will go."

"Where?" Sean asked, rubbing the back of his neck.

"They go to Rio Bravo. A small village. But there is a *médico* in Rio Bravo. A doctor."

"How far from here?"

"Only about four miles."

Sean thought a moment. Attempting a rescue would be foolhardy, but his rage continued to burn. Sean also wondered how the kidnapping of Señorita del Carmen might affect his business south of the border.

"Can you show me the way, Paco?"

"*Sí*, Señor."

"Mr. Black, I want you to get this boat off this sandbar and return the chaperone to Matamoros. Then go to Brownsville, get the smaller boat and return here to Devil's Elbow. Mr. Koch, round up two rifles, some jerky and three canteens of water. You and I are going to fetch Miss del Carmen. We'll rendezvous here tomorrow afternoon."

The country around Devil's Elbow was bathed in yellow light from the setting sun. Two men and a boy dropped from the rail of the *James H. Dawkins* and splashed up the riverbank into Mexico.

"We can run, then walk," Paco suggested.

"Sounds good," Sean said, his heart already pounding with excitement. "Let's go!"

The trio trotted south across butterscotch-colored clay, through the prickly pear cacti and yucca plants. A pair of turkey vultures wheeled above.

Paco looked back and saw both men had fallen about 40 feet behind. He slowed to a walk, glancing about the dirt as he went. Suddenly, he stopped.

"Señor Darragh, look!" Paco cried as Sean and Koch walked up, still panting. "Horses came along here. You can see their tracks."

Paco bent over and walked slowly. A moment later, he found what he sought, a small splat of blood from the wounded bandit. The drop had hit a thick leaf of an agave plant. "It's them," Paco said with conviction.

"Good work, Paco," Sean said. "Let's trot again."

Evening descended across the badlands as the threesome resumed their run toward Rio Bravo. They had made only 400 yards when Koch hit a large rock and pitched forward.

"Ayeee!" Koch cried as his foot turned. Paco and Sean backtracked to their companion who was now sitting up, rubbing his ankle.

"How bad is it, Glen?" Sean asked.

"I'm all right," Koch insisted as he gathered his rifle and hobbled to his feet. "Let's go."

"Señor, Rio Bravo is only about two hours if we walk," Paco advised.

"That'll get us there by at least 10 o'clock," Sean mused. "Running in the dark isn't worth the risk. Let's walk it."

A quarter moon provided precious little light, and nettles pulled at Sean's trousers. As the group of unlikely rescuers trod through the sand and brush, Sean began to wonder if he had made a mistake. How were two gringos and a boy going to walk into a Mexican village, find a young woman, subdue her captors and escape back into the night? Sean had no plan, but he had determination, one partner and Paco. That might be enough.

He wondered why the bandits would take the girl and nothing else. He wondered if the bandits were waiting in ambush. Then as the trio topped a small hill, Paco spotted the clay huts and three small adobe buildings that were Rio Bravo. They were only 600 yards from the village.

"What now?" Sean asked aloud.

"Let me go into the village," Paco suggested. "I will find out what I can and come back to you."

Koch was suspicious. "How do we know you're not in cahoots with these bandits?" he charged.

"Leave him alone," Sean interrupted. "OK, Paco, let's go up to those rocks. Glen and I will wait for you there. If you're not back in one hour, we're coming in. Here, take my watch."

"*Sí*, Señor," Paco agreed. "I will return in one hour."

Sean and Koch took turns keeping watch over the rock. Koch's ankle was getting stiff, but he didn't complain. He stretched out his legs and closed his eyes. Sean heard the first snore and turned to wake him. That's when he saw the rattlesnake slithering over Koch's boot.

Sean gasped and froze. The 5-foot serpent glided across Koch's boot, then stopped and coiled. Sean slowly eased his pistol from its holster and pulled the lever. Could he risk the noise of a gunshot? He prayed Glen wouldn't move.

Koch continued to snore. The snake was coiled beside his leg, but it didn't seem interested in Glen. Its head was motionless, its yellow eyes locked on a nearby rock. Sean pointed his pistol at the rattler with two trembling hands. In one instant, he heard a noise from the village and turned to look. In the next instant, the rattler struck its target.

When Sean looked back, the snake had a small field mouse in its mouth. He watched with fascination as the mouse disappeared. Once the rattler swallowed the mouse, it slowly slithered off. Sean uncocked his pistol and blew a huge sigh. Koch stirred, but kept snoring. Sean decided to let him sleep.

"Señor Darragh," Paco's voice came in a loud whisper from the other side of the rocks. It startled Sean. He jolted around and pulled his pistol. Koch woke with a snort.

"Paco?" Sean whispered back.

"*Sí*, it is Paco." The boy crawled past a large rock and crouched next to the men. Holding Sean's watch out to him, Paco reported, "Señor Darragh, I found them. Señorita del

An Unlikely Group of Rescuers

Carmen is in the village. One bandito is dead. The other drinks at the cantina. Cheo is with the señorita in a small hut at the edge of the village."

"Cheo?" Sean asked. "Who is Cheo?"

"He is a very brave and dangerous bandito. The people of the village fear Cheo, but they like him. He gives people money and things he has stolen. He is alone with the señorita."

Paco's eyes glowed with excitement. "If we can surprise Cheo during the night, we might get the señorita back and escape without detection."

"Paco, if we pull this off and get out alive, I want you to come work for me," Sean grinned. "Now, let's figure how we'll turn the tables on this Cheo."

Just To Be Together

S ean Darragh's plan to rescue Catharine del Carmen was simple. Once her abductor, Cheo Flores, was asleep in the hut, Sean would enter, knock him unconscious and tie him. Then he'd take the señorita back to the Rio Grande.

In the late night stillness, Sean turned to Paco, the young Mexican servant. "Do you think you could sneak back into the village and steal as many as three horses?"

"I don't know, Señor Darragh," the boy answered. "But I will try."

"If you can, bring them back and we'll meet you here after we get Señorita del Carmen out. I'd like to be under cover back at the river before anyone here discovers what's happened."

As Sean was planning his rescue attempt, the *James H. Dawkins* landed at Brownsville. Standing at the dock was a young woman accompanied by a man who leaned on a cane. It was dark, and both looked anxiously toward the light in the wheelhouse, trying to spot a familiar face. The crewmen worked quickly. None were smiling.

Robert Black hustled down the landing plank. As he stepped ashore, the man asked, "Where is Sean Darragh?"

Black was about to pass, but the man blocked his path

with his cane. Black was annoyed. "Who wants to know?"

"Someone who has business with him," Cleve Everline answered. "I'm with the Pinkerton Detective Agency, and we've come from New York to find him. This is his boat. Now, where is he?"

Everline's accident had taken its toll on his body but not his spirit. Black could easily have pushed the man aside, but Everline was the one in control. Black figured he shouldn't take this man lightly.

"He's in Mexico. We had some trouble on the way to Reynosa. I'm getting a smaller boat to go back and pick him up."

"We'll go with you," Everline said.

"No, sir, we can't take any passengers."

"Then we'll go as crew. I'm the best marksman you'll find. And this young lady grew up on a steamboat. If we don't go with you, we'll be right behind you in another boat."

Black studied their determined faces. He paused a moment, then said with resignation, "OK, you can come."

Rio Bravo slept under a clear black sky full of stars. It was peaceful, save for the two men who staggered toward a hut on the edge of town. Sean had found an empty bottle. If he and Glen Koch were spotted, a couple of drunks would arouse less suspicion than two men sneaking about.

They were only 20 feet from the hut when Sean heard muffled Spanish voices. Suddenly a shutter flew open.

"*¿Que pasó?*" Cheo barked.

Sean lurched forward with his bottle and said in slurred Spanish, "*Nada. Nada. Lo siento, Señor.*"

He put an arm around Glen's shoulders, and the pair staggered down the path.

The shutters closed. They moved a few paces farther, then

circled back to the boulders just outside the village.

"Whew, that was close!" Koch breathed heavily.

"Too close," Sean agreed. "Looks like we'll have to wait a few hours more."

Suddenly, they heard the steps of horses. Wheeling around, they spied Paco riding one mare and leading another. He slipped quietly from the horse's back.

"Good work, Paco," Sean said.

"*¿Donde está la Señorita del Carmen?*" Paco asked.

"Cheo was still awake," Sean answered. "We could hear them talking. Paco, does Catharine know him?"

"No, I don't think so."

"Well, I couldn't make out what they were saying, but they sounded friendly."

It was nearly dawn before Sean and Koch set out again. This time they didn't fake being drunk. They snuck quietly to the hut. Koch, his pistol drawn, stood near the window.

Sean went to the door and tried the latch. Locked. He motioned to Koch, then leveled his rifle and kicked hard at the door. It gave easily, and he burst through the doorway.

"*¡Levanta las manos!*" he cried, pointing his rifle at Cheo. The Mexican bolted up, wide-eyed, beside his bed. He saw Sean's rifle, glanced back at the pistol in his holster and slowly raised his hands.

"*¡No! ¡No!*" came a voice from the wall. It was Catharine. In two quick steps, she moved in front of Cheo. She was terrified, but held up her hands as though they might shield him from Sean's bullets.

Sean stood there, dumbfounded.

"*Señor, no. Por favor. Déjenos en paz,*" Catharine implored.

In that moment, Sean thought of Ann Sessions and how she had protected him from the Pinkerton detective. Now

Catharine was doing the same for Cheo. Sean thought it useless to rescue Catharine if she didn't want to be rescued. He shook his head slowly, sighed and lowered his rifle.

"I thought you were kidnapped," he said softly. "I didn't know."

Cheo answered as he put his hands on Catharine's shoulders. "We only made it look like kidnap, Señor. We want to marry, but her father will never allow it."

Sean thought a moment. "Then I'll return and tell him I was unable to locate her."

"Thank you," Cheo murmured. "You are a good man. I am sorry I hit you."

Sean grinned and rubbed his sore head. "So am I."

There was no rush to return to the river. Sean, Koch and Paco walked to the cantina with Cheo and Catharine. They ate a breakfast of tortillas, eggs and coffee. They talked of the war, Sean's business and Cheo's land.

"Señor Darragh, would you buy my land? Catharine and I need the money, and the land is of no use to me."

Sean gulped and asked the price. Cheo shrugged and suggested $1,000. It came to less than 2 cents an acre.

"Yes, Cheo, I would like to buy your land. I can bring you the money next week."

At noon, the party rode to the bend in the Rio Grande called Codo del Diablo. Within the hour, a 30-foot scow steamed up the river. Several of its crew held rifles at the ready as it nosed to the Mexican shore. Sean began waving a white handkerchief as a sign of no danger. Then he saw Cleve Everline sitting against the cabin, a rifle in his lap.

Sean cocked his rifle and called out, "Mr. Everline, you are the last person I expected to see out here. State your business, sir."

"I came to help, not to arrest you," Everline said evenly. Then he grinned and added in a more gentle tone, "I also brought someone with me."

Ann Sessions appeared smiling at the cabin door and said softly, "Hello, Sean. Remember me?"

The scow steamed southeast, back to Brownsville. As evening shadows lengthened across the river, Ann and Everline took turns telling Sean about the incident that triggered his journey to Texas. Sean was innocent of Mike Fenwick's death. The shot didn't even come from the pistol they fought over during the struggle. The fatal bullet was from another's gun, one of the thugs Fenwick knew. The killer confessed to the crime shortly before he was hanged for a second murder.

"You're no killer, Sean." Everline said. "And because you rescued me after the explosion on the Mississippi, I wanted to tell you in person."

"And I wanted to see your face when he told you," Ann teased.

"Is that the only reason you came with him?" Sean asked with a slight smile.

Ann tilted her head and stuck out her chin. "Of course," she managed with a pout.

Sean clasped Ann's waist and pulled her to him.

"Ann, I always thought I had to make something of myself before I could court you. Now I've met two young Mexicans who would live as fugitives in poverty if they could just be together. I may not be a killer, but I am a fool who did not act on his feelings when he should have. Will you give me one more chance?"

"Just one, Sean Darragh," Ann smiled as she studied his eyes. "Just one."

River Run
To Texas
Part II

Carlos and Veronica

*C*arlos del Carmen rose from his afternoon siesta, walked to his dresser and splashed cool water on his rugged face. For a few moments, he leaned against the dresser with his massive hands on either side of the water bowl. Not yet fully awake, he scooped up more water and splashed again. That would have to do. He toweled himself dry, then raked the towel across the puddles around the bowl.

Carlos stretched and walked out onto the veranda where he surveyed his rancho, Los Cazaderos. As usual, he was among the first to stir after siesta. The only sign of life below was the old vaquero, Francisco, who silently braided a rawhide reata in the shade of an ironwood tree. Carlos' gaze swept across the courtyard to the wall framing the yard's north side.

The headquarters of his rancho dominated the crest of a small hill, presenting a view of a quarter of his holdings from his office veranda. Today, across miles of saw grass, agave and spiny cacti, he spotted a tiny wisp of dust rising from the dun-colored earth near the horizon. The blot of dust was too far away to discern what created it. Maybe it was just a dust devil. Perhaps it heralded a visitor or one of his vaqueros riding back to the headquarters.

With its three buildings and walled enclosure, headquarters was more a fortress than a home. One building was the stable with some livestock, a tack room and a storeroom. Opposite it was another building of equal size that was home to the servants and their families.

The Great House completed the large rectangle. It contained 28 rooms, including a dozen guest rooms, two kitchens, two dining rooms, the master suite, a library, offices and sitting rooms. All this for one man and his daughter, Catharine.

Catharine's mother, Veronica, had died giving birth to her first child. Carlos never remarried, instead turning his passion to the business of ranching. His was the fourth generation to own Los Cazaderos. The land was granted to his great-grandfather for service as an officer in the Spanish armada.

If anything, Carlos felt guilty for having the good fortune to be born to such wealth. He assuaged the guilt by working hard to expand and improve his property.

Now Carlos could see the wisp of dust framed the silhouette of a man on horseback.

After his wife's death, Carlos provided his daughter with the best nursemaids, the most knowledgeable tutors and always plenty of competent servants.

But he could not give her the best of himself. The pain of his loss burned so deeply, he could never speak Veronica's name. At a very young age, Catharine learned any mention of her mother caused her father's jaw to tighten, or worse, to launch into a fit of rage.

Carlos loved his daughter, that was clear to her and everyone around them, but Carlos turned to stone at the mention of his dear departed wife. What little Catharine knew of Veronica, she learned mostly from reading family records and listening to stories told by the servants who swore her to secrecy lest they incur her father's wrath.

The lone rider was closer now and riding at a gallop. A narrow-brimmed sombrero with a cone-shaped crown suggested a young rider, and Carlos made a mental note to have someone speak to the youthful vaquero about pushing his horse in the midday heat.

Carlos returned to his desk to study a map of Los Cazaderos and several surrounding ranches. His forefinger traced a line of blue ink highlighting the boundary between his rancho and that of the Gutierrez family.

The Gutierrez holdings were only about a fourth of the del Carmen rancho, but their land lay west of Los Cazaderos. Although Carlos was able to bring water from Rio San Juan, the Gutierrez land included a larger river, Rio Pesqueria.

With water nearly as precious as gold, controlling water rights by uniting the two ranchos would secure the livelihoods of the two ranchos and increase their value.

That union would be achieved through the forthcoming marriage of his daughter Catharine to Guillermo Gutierrez, the heir to the family's holdings.

Carlos had known Guillermo's father, Hector, since childhood. Thirty miles of desert between their respective homes kept them from being close friends, but they were on good neighborly terms.

It was Hector who proposed an arranged marriage between their children. Carlos considered the proposal carefully as he watched his Catharine mature into a charming young lady. Each day she became more beautiful, more like his Veronica years ago.

Yes, it must be so, Carlos declared.

"I have found for you a husband, and his father agrees to the union," Carlos announced happily. "After a courtship of six months, you will be wed to Guillermo Gutierrez."

"No!" she shrieked. "No! No!" With each "No," her voice became less of a scream and more of a sobbing whine and finally, a moan of desperation.

"I thought you would be pleased," muttered her bewildered father.

"Pleased? Oh, Papa, how could you?"

Catharine cried for days, but Carlos stood fast. He remained convinced the arranged marriage and its promise of future wealth and security would be in the best interests of his daughter.

What does she know of love? Guillermo is a good man and reliable. "The courtship will change her mind. She will see."

A shout interrupted his daydreaming. Carlos strode back to the veranda. Now he could hear the thumping hoofbeats of the rider's mount and more shouting to open the gate. Francisco shuffled toward the entrance to open the gate. The rider dismounted, shaking and stretching his legs.

"Hurry, old man," snapped the rider.

Carlos felt a blanket of dread being pulled over his body. His palms began to sweat, and his face became red and tight. The fear was as sure and cold as death itself.

He wheeled and walked briskly through the office and down the stairway. An urgent pounding beat him to his front door. Carlos pulled the door to him to reveal the young rider, sweaty and panting.

He had covered 30 miles since dawn and now that he faced his patron, he gulped and choked as he tried to speak.

"Well, what is it?" demanded Carlos.

The frightened messenger could not bear to meet the dread in the eyes of Señor del Carmen. Instead, he focused on a button of his shirt and blurted, "It is your daughter, Señor. She was kidnapped from the steamboat. Her chaperone reports it was the act of the bandito known as Cheo."

Carlos looked past the messenger to Francisco hovering in the door. "Gather the men," he barked. Then, to the messenger, he ordered, "Get help for your horse at the stable and return here. We need every detail you can remember. Hurry."

As Carlos shut the door, the two men scurried to carry out their orders. The noise from inside stopped them in their tracks.

A sound, a wail, a shriek, some cry that couldn't be made

by a human. Surely it was the scream of a wounded animal. The old man knew it wasn't. He shut his eyes in pain, crossed himself, then hurried to ring the bell.

With Love and Grace

I do."

Sean's vow echoed off the tiled office walls at the Nueces County Courthouse in Corpus Christi. The boom of his own voice surprised Sean, as though the words came from someone else. He was consumed with joy, soaking in each word, glance and detail, to remember the moments forever. The harder he tried to concentrate, the more his mind was overwhelmed with the love he felt for his bride.

Ann stood by Sean's side, dressed in her best gown, a periwinkle blue silk dress her father brought to Texas for the wedding. It was not a wedding gown, but suitable for such a ceremony, especially in the vast frontier that was Texas. For Ann, the dress had the greatest of sentimental value. It had once belonged to her departed mother.

As Ann stood before a mirror, preparing for the ceremony, she tried to imagine how her mother might have looked in it. She smoothed the fabric of the waist length bodice and the full length skirt. She fiddled with the lace trim around the neck. As she did so, Ann imagined her mother's embrace, her warmth, even her scent. In those moments before the ceremony, her mother was once again alive and by her side.

Now Ann was smiling at the promise of Sean's words echoing and tumbling through the future when she would work by his side, carving out a life together on the coastal plains of Texas.

It was not the kind of life Ann had envisioned for herself. She was born to the river and always thought her life would somehow be connected to the waterways of America. However, she now was perfectly willing to give up her life on a steamboat for this land of promise and a life with young Sean Darragh.

"Ann, will you take Sean Darragh as your husband, to love, honor and cherish?" the justice of the peace asked.

Her life with this young Irishman on their ranch in southern Texas would be on a harsh and unforgiving land.

She looked into Sean's eyes with a gentle smile and without hesitation, answered, "I do," in a strong, clear voice that echoed as well.

"I pronounce you man and wife."

Sean cupped Ann's face in his hands, and their lips met tenderly in a deep kiss. As she returned his embrace, Ann whispered, "*Now* you may call me Annie."

The young couple's wedding was not a big, grandiose event, but it was not untypical of the majority of nuptials in the early days of Texas statehood. Such ceremonies were, by necessity, direct and expedient. Only the wealthy or old aristocratic families with plenty of spare time could afford the luxury of an elaborate church wedding.

It mattered not to Annie. She was a woman now, not a girl who pined for the frivolous. Her feelings of love and passion for Sean were as strong as the river currents that had brought their lives together.

The Nueces County Courthouse would not have been Annie's first choice for a wedding site, but it was convenient. Besides, with the abundance of tile, the courthouse had an exotic, even romantic quality. A steady breeze rattled the palms outside the open windows of the crowded office.

Although the ceremony was modest, it attracted a circle of family, friends and well-wishers. Joseph Sessions gladly gave his daughter's hand in marriage. Upon hearing the news, he had quickly steamed down the Ohio and Mississippi rivers and sailed across the Gulf of Mexico with his brother, Noble, and Noble's wife, Viola, to witness the union and wish the young couple well.

Sean had wired the news of his pending matrimony to his brother, Ty Darragh, in Ireland. It would have taken at least two months for Ty to make the trip across the Atlantic, so standing in for Ty as best man was Cleve Everline, the Pinkerton detective who had once vowed to bring Sean to justice.

Despite the danger of being discovered, another young couple attended – Cheo and Catharine. Without his pistols and bandoliers, and disguised in a plain brown suit, Cheo looked nothing like a bandito. Instead, he appeared to the many Texans walking the streets of Corpus Christi as a respected Mexican businessman. He and Catharine brought Paco with them. Other friends from Sean's steamboat business in Brownsville filled the office and followed the couple to the reception back at the bayfront hotel.

Early in the evening, waiters lit the oil lamps on the hotel veranda where three musicians strummed guitars and sang notes of love songs.

Joseph Sessions called the couple to his side and presented a gilded walnut box to Sean. Annie smiled at her new husband as Sean fumbled to open the ornate catch. He lifted the lid to reveal a gold compass, its patina burnished by careful use.

"This compass has been in our family for three generations," Joseph said. "It has guided our family on straight and narrow courses. My brother Noble and I now want to pass it along to you with our prayers that no matter what your future brings, you find your way with love and grace."

Later, Cheo toasted Sean and Annie. "Is everything set for your purchase of my land tomorrow?"

"Yes," Sean nodded. "The land commissioner's office is just down the hall from where we had the wedding. Are you sure it's safe for you to be here?"

"Nowhere is safe for us now," answered Cheo, who put a protective arm around Catharine's shoulders. "Her father has offered a reward for my capture and Catharine's return. I have two friends keeping watch outside. I think Carlos will look for us first in Mexico."

Sean shifted uncomfortably, his gaze wandering everywhere but directly in his friend's eyes. "Cheo, I don't ... uh, I don't feel, well, right about paying such a low price for Santa Estefana. I think your land may be worth three times the price you're selling it to us."

"Do not worry, *mi amigo*. I own other land south of the Rio Grande, and I have no use for the grant I sell to you. If it is worth more, then consider the balance as our wedding gift to you both."

"Cheo, you are a remarkable man. I hope you and Catharine will come visit us when you are able."

Cleve Everline silently joined the two couples. He leaned against his cane and occasionally touched his drink to his lips, but he drank little. He looked tired and drawn but managed a slight grin as the young couples discussed Sean's new ranch.

"I'd offer to go with you in case there's trouble, but I should be returning to New York," said Everline. "Besides, you can handle trouble. I've seen evidence of that."

"Mr. Everline, there is one thing you might help me with before you leave," suggested Sean.

"What's that?"

"Teach me how to use a pistol and rifle. I hardly know anything about weapons, and I may need to use them in defense of my property."

"Teach me, too!" Ann quickly added. Then, as looks of surprise and amusement were shared among the group, Ann lifted her chin defiantly and grabbed Sean's arm, spilling some of his drink. "*I* may need to defend my property!"

A Mexican waiter appeared from nowhere and used a small towel to blot the drink from the floor. He raised up and, for the first time, noticed Cheo. His eyes flickered in surprise, but he quickly regained his composure and offered to replace Sean's drink. Sean waved him away with a smile, unaware his friend's safety had been compromised.

Had Cheo noticed, the waiter wondered. The man tried not to appear in a hurry as he headed back to the kitchen. Once he cleared the swinging doors, he broke into a trot that carried him out the back door and two blocks down the street. He bounded up wooden stairs that led to a communal flat and burst through the doors. The five men grumbled as they looked up from their card game. But the news could lead to a wealthy reward, even split six ways, if only for the time it took one to drink and gamble it away.

"*¡Amigos, el bandito Cheo es aquí en Corpus Christi!*"

The men dropped their cards and reached for hats and holsters.

Love and Betrayal

*A*s the music and laughter of the wedding reception spilled from the bayfront hotel into the cool evening, six men fanned out across the dusty streets of Corpus Christi. Each was nervous, trying to be nonchalant, but walking far too quickly. It was only two blocks, but for two men, it might as well have been two miles.

Ernesto was tall, but fat and slow. He thought only of his share of the reward for returning Catharine del Carmen to her father in Mexico. It would keep him in mescal, tequila and cigars for a long, long time. His heavy spurs sounded a steady *chink ... chink ... chink* on the boardwalks. *Better move to the road to avoid noise*, Ernesto thought.

As he stumbled forward, the toe of his boot caught a wooden plank, pitching the huge man forward. His left kneecap crashed down on a large flat rock.

"AYAIIIIII!" Ernesto screamed as the pain seared through his knee.

Ernesto's brother emerged from the darkness, muttering curses as he helped Ernesto to his feet. Ernesto whimpered and moaned. His leg would not carry him, so he leaned heavily as his brother edged him back to the room.

Reuben was equally unlucky. In his rush to join his comrades, he forgot about the effects of the beer and tequila he had consumed earlier. He was drunk, to be sure, but not so drunk he was unaware of the need to relieve himself. He came upon a narrow alley and ducked in. Unfortunately, a sheriff's deputy walked out of his boardinghouse and discovered Reuben and his indiscretion. He loosened the strap over his pistol but left it in his holster.

"OK, amigo. Button up and let's go," said the deputy, motioning Reuben over.

Reuben spoke quickly, "*Pardon, Señor, pardon. Pero lo ere necessario. Muy necessario.*"

Reuben continued talking excitedly in Spanish, most of which the Texas deputy could not decipher. What he did understand was the sheriff's crackdown on such loose behavior, and he figured his boss would be pleased his young deputy was enforcing the ordinance.

The deputy grabbed Reuben roughly with his left arm, leaving his right for the pistol, if necessary.

Reuben, not wanting to cause a commotion that would deter his friends from their goal of capturing Catharine and Cheo, obliged and shuffled off to spend the night in jail. Three down, three left.

Miguel, the waiter, had rushed ahead of the group to size up the situation inside. As he snuck back out of the hotel, Miguel saw only two men.

In a hoarse whisper, he croaked, "What happened to the others?"

The attempted explanation drew an angry retort, "Idiots." Miguel threw up his hands. "Let's watch the hotel and we'll capture them tomorrow."

The window curtains of Sean and Annie's room slow-danced in a steady gulf breeze. The first ray of sun crept over the sill and onto Sean's face. He awoke without movement, and his eyes focused on Annie's face, just a few inches from his. She looked earnest in slumber, her mouth partly open and her cheeks flushed with the morning warmth.

Sean studied her countenance and pondered their future together. Life on a ranch would be like nothing the young couple had ever experienced, but Sean was confident they could make it work.

Ever since Cheo had offered his land for sale, Sean had been reading every book he could find about ranching. He knew there was already a good demand for beef from the Northern states. But he had something more in mind. He would begin by breeding stock so he would be ready when the railroads pushed through the Midwest and Southwest.

If they were successful, Sean and Annie could amass a fortune. Or they might end up dead. Local sheriffs provided the only law enforcement, and their ranch was at least 50 miles from the nearest town. The Corpus Christi company of Texas Rangers had disbanded a year ago. Indian raids, while not common, still were reported from time to time.

Suddenly apprehension closed in on Sean.

Was this fair to Annie? Was he dragging her into a life she would hate? Would she grow to resent his schemes and failures as a Texas rancher?

He brushed a ringlet of dark hair from her cheek. Annie blinked and opened her eyes. They sparkled immediately into a warm smile.

"Good morning, Mrs. Darragh," whispered Sean.

"Aye, Mr. Darragh, 'tis a very good morning indeed," answered his young wife as she snuggled close to him.

Sean held her in his arms, the apprehension sliding away with his sigh. He knew full well she was strong enough for the life that awaited them.

The gulf breeze continued its waltz, ruffling the tablecloths on the veranda where the Darraghs shared breakfast with Cheo and Catharine.

Waiters brought pitchers of juice and plates of eggs, bacon, fruit and tortillas. Conversation was pleasant, despite being slowed by the need to translate for Catharine.

Other wedding guests began filing down to the veranda, and last night's reception seemed to pick up where it had left off.

"Señora Darragh," said Cheo, "I do not wish to impose, but would you stay with Catharine and Paco while your husband and I settle our business at the courthouse? She was ill earlier this morning. We should not be long."

"Of course," answered Annie. "My family will be leaving later this afternoon, so we'll just stay out here and enjoy the day with them."

Cheo translated and Catharine flashed a smile. "*Gracias*," she said.

Sean and Annie's wedding marked the first time in a while that Catharine had felt like a normal person and not a woman on the run partnered with a known bandit.

She relished her time at the luxurious hotel with her lover. Ann's relatives and even the sinister-looking Cleve Everline were very nice to her. She understood only what was literally translated for her, but the friendliness of the Sessions family reached across the language barrier and extended feelings of warmth and belonging to Catharine.

She wondered about her father. Surely he was enraged and disappointed in her. Catharine hoped there would come a day when she might reconcile with her father. But for now she was perfectly happy to be at the side of Cheo, the young rebel who broke with his own family and once rode for Catharine's father, Carlos.

Catharine smiled as memories of that time rushed back. Cheo was her bodyguard. He and another guard would accompany the señorita on all her rides. Cheo would take the lead, and the other guard would follow behind. She was attracted to the handsome and dashing horseman but tried her best not to show it. For his part, Cheo was so enchanted by Catharine, he could not chance a look into her eyes, lest he blush and stammer.

An accident brought them together.

Her horse, spooked by a snake, bucked her off, then fell down in a gully and broke its leg. Cheo swung his mount around, spurred the animal and pulled up in a cloud of dust.

"Señorita, Señorita, are you hurt?" he shouted as he dismounted and ran frantically to her side. She touched his shoulder. "I'm fine. Just a little shaken. Can you help me up?"

"All I saw was your horse, and I feared the worst."

"Calm down, Cheo, I'm all right now that you're here."

Cheo gathered her up in his arms and carried her to his horse. He moistened his bandanna with cold water from his canteen and dabbed her warm cheeks. Only when her cheeks blushed pink from his adoring stare did he release her.

Cheo lifted her gently onto his horse and turned toward the house. "Manuel," he shouted to the other guard, "take care of her stallion."

When the shot rang out, Catharine began sobbing. Cheo lifted her from the saddle and held her tenderly. As Catharine's sobs grew quieter, her arms slid around Cheo's neck. Her eyes met his, and she brushed her lips ever so slightly on his. At that moment, they both knew they could no longer deny their love for each other.

Cheo knew her father would never allow a courtship between the two. That evening, he went to Señor del Carmen and resigned his post, saying only that he was going back to his family.

Cheo rode away at twilight, but not before leaving a note

in Catharine's saddlebags promising he would someday return for her. She had discovered it that day as she searched for some message to explain his absence. Her response was swift and everlasting. She would wait for him.

Now the handsome young man she loved sat next to her, occasionally patting her hand or gently touching her shoulder. He was attentive, but not patronizing. Although Catharine was the only one there who could not speak English, Cheo made certain she was part of every conversation, placing Paco on her other side so the young boy could translate whenever Cheo was speaking English.

"Señor Darragh, it is time for us to visit the courthouse," Cheo announced. "I would like to finish our transaction early, if possible. Catharine and I must leave soon. We must stay on the move."

"The land commission office should be open by now," replied Sean. "First, I should say my goodbyes to Annie's folks. It won't take but a few minutes."

Sean and Annie moved from table to table, accepting congratulations and making promises to visit as soon as they could. The Sessions family was ready to leave for the docks as well, so more farewells mixed with the sounds of chairs scraping across the satillo tile.

As Cheo and Sean left the hotel for the courthouse, neither saw the whittler across the street fold his knife and begin walking in the same direction.

Love and Betrayal

Gunfight and Capture

*T*he county clerk added his signature to those of Cheo and Sean and blew across the damp ink. As he affixed the official seal, he looked up at the two men across the polished wooden counter, and announced, "Gentlemen, we're all done. Congratulations on your transaction."

Sean and Cheo shook hands. "Now you are a landowner," said Cheo, slapping the new owner on the back. "How does it feel, amigo?"

"Feels good, but a bit scary at the same time," admitted Sean as they walked, papers in hand, down the hallway of the Nueces County Courthouse. "I hope it all works out, for us, and for you and Catharine."

Cheo chewed on his lip and nodded. "It will work out ... somehow it will."

As they crossed the lobby, their footsteps echoing through the hallway, the main door to the courthouse banged opened. One of Cheo's guards staggered through, clutching his side. He stumbled to his knees, then pitched forward. One hand was covered with blood. Somewhere in the melee, a woman screamed as the two men rushed to the fallen guard.

"Run, Señor!" he rasped. "They come for you."

Cheo turned sharply and looked through the doorway. Three men were trotting up the steps. One held a knife. Sean suddenly felt cold, chilled by his old fugitive fears. He grabbed Cheo's arm. "Let's try the back door."

Cheo jumped to his feet and dashed down the hallway, Sean on his heels. Several people began emerging from their offices, drawn by the commotion. The fallen guard pulled his pistol, rose to his knees and fired through the front door. The report was deafening. The smell of black powder wafted through the lobby a split second before pandemonium broke out. A return hail of gunfire sent the guard sprawling in the throes of death.

They were 20 feet from the back of the courthouse when the door swung open and a man leveled his gun at Cheo and Sean. Cheo pushed Sean through an office door just as the man fired. The shot splintered the doorjamb as Cheo slammed the door shut and locked it.

A woman screamed and began swinging her purse in the general direction of the two men. Another man in the office tried to wedge himself behind a filing cabinet but succeeded only in turning it over and sending a flurry of papers in every direction. The attacker was now beating against the heavy solid door.

Sean grabbed the woman and hissed, "Stop it, woman. We mean you no harm." She bit him on the wrist and struggled free.

Cheo pushed open the shutters to the office window and hollered, "This way, Sean!"

The lithe Mexican climbed out the window, Sean close behind. The pair found themselves in an alley. Which way to run? People scurried up and down the street. Some were armed. The two men looked anxiously one way and then the other.

Who was after them? Where was the sheriff? Who were the good guys? Who were the bad?

Sean saw an empty corner. "Let's try this way." They were in luck. The alley came out on another street. They could hear shouts and saw people ducking into buildings, but the coast looked clear.

Gasping for air, Sean confessed, "Cheo, I left my pistol back at the hotel!"

"No matter, my friend. They may need it more than us."

At the hotel several blocks away, Paco heard the first inkling of danger. He was on the landing at the top of the stairs, watching people go through the lobby when he heard the distant gunfire. At the same time he noticed an armed man enter the lobby. The man waved his pistol about the lobby nervously, then started up the steps. Paco rushed to Sean and Annie's room and warned the women a man was coming for them.

Annie grabbed her husband's gun and ordered Paco to find Cleve Everline. She latched the door, grabbed Catharine by the wrist and pulled her behind the bed. Annie's heart was pounding, but she calmly checked the pistol to ensure it was loaded, pulled the hammer back to cock it, then pointed it toward the door.

Everline was standing at his water basin, shaving, when Paco began pounding on his door. He had barely opened his door when Paco shouted.

"Señor, come quickly! Señora Darragh is in danger!"

Without wiping the shaving cream from his face, Everline pulled his holster from the bedpost and followed Paco down the hallway. They came to a turn in the hallway and found a man at Annie's door with a gun drawn. Everline pulled Paco back with one hand, pulled his weapon with the other and ordered, "Drop the pistol!"

The man wheeled and fired, the shot whizzing to a stop in the wall. Everline never flinched. He calmly squeezed off one well-calculated shot that struck the man in the breast. The gunman grunted and fell back into a sitting position, then slumped over dead.

"Stay back, Paco!" Everline leveled his gun at the body until he could retrieve the weapon, then called through the closed door, "Miss Sessions, uh, Mrs. Darragh, it's Cleve Everline! Are you and the señorita all right?"

In a moment, the door cracked open and Annie's face appeared. "Yes, Mr. Everline. Thank you for coming. You saved our lives."

"You two stay inside. I'll remain here, and Paco will summon the sheriff. Understood?"

"Yes. Thank you again."

Catharine was still backed into a corner. She couldn't understand the language, but she knew full well what was happening. Someone was trying to collect her father's reward. Panic welled inside her as she thought of her young lover. Where was Cheo? Was he safe?

In the confusion outside, Sean and Cheo crossed the street undetected and headed back toward the hotel. They were only a block away when two men opened fire on them. They ducked into an alley. As Cheo covered him, Sean ran to the other end of the alley looking for an escape. He reached the end and looked one way. It was a dead end. He looked the other way into a dark hole that was the muzzle of a man's pistol.

"*Alto*," came the man's command. Sean stopped, as ordered. "Turn around." A gun jabbed his back. "Forward." Sean took several steps then. Cheo looked back to discover Sean's capture. Two more men closed in on Cheo from the street.

"Señor Flores, drop your pistol or your friend will be shot."

Cheo weighed his options for a split second as Sean's

captor pulled the hammer back on his pistol. Cheo tossed his weapon into the sand and stood with his hands raised. The two men joined them in the alley. The one who captured Sean faced Sean and Cheo and ordered the other two to tie their hands.

Sean studied the man's face. "I've seen you before, but where? Where? Ah, last night at the reception! You were the waiter who cleaned up the drink I spilled!"

"Señor Flores, you are going to bring us a great deal of money," said the waiter.

"*I* can pay you a great deal of money for our freedom, and you won't have to take me to Mexico to collect it," offered Cheo.

"You are a kidnapper and bandit who has no money and even if you had it, I would never be able to spend it once Señor del Carmen learned I had you and his daughter, then released you."

The man nodded to his partners behind Sean and Cheo. Their pistols swung downward, and Sean and Cheo fell motionless to the ground.

Kidnapped

*A*s the haze lifted slowly, Sean found himself lying on a wooden floor. Something had caused him to roll over. Cheo's still body was partly over his. They lay in a heap, a horrible smell putrefying the air.

Sean felt himself being lifted, then falling again. As his eyes finally focused, he saw light coming through hundreds of tiny squares. He heard a groan, but it wasn't human. It was the groaning of wood and fittings. They were on a boat! The way the vessel pitched and bobbed, he was sure they were not on a river. They had to be somewhere in the ocean. Of course! The Gulf of Mexico!

Projecting from the size of the hold where they lay, Sean figured they were aboard a sloop, most likely a fishing boat judging from the smell. He figured the craft was not large, maybe 30 feet long and very wide abeam. There were no voices topside, only the occasional flap of sail and the constant sound of water flowing past the hull.

"Where are we headed?" Sean asked himself. Looking through the hatch, he could see the boom. "OK, they're on a beat. The prevailing winds are from the south, so it's a good bet we're headed down the coast, maybe toward Brownsville or maybe farther south to the Mexican coast."

Sean struggled to move free of Cheo, but his hands and feet were tied. He noticed a dark stain. Blood had seeped into a few of the wooden planks. Was it his or Cheo's? His

Mexican friend lay facedown now. His jet black hair was matted and still wet with blood.

Sean studied Cheo's body. Cheo was still breathing, but he had not made a sound, not even a moan or a snore, in the few moments Sean had been conscious. His head was turned away. His hands and feet were tied. His brown wedding suit was now torn and filthy.

"Annie!" his heart screamed silently. Was she safe, or had she and Catharine been captured as well? There was no way to tell, but perhaps they were safe. If they had been captured, they would probably be sharing the same wretched quarters as Cheo and himself. Or if their captors were humane, the women would be topside or perhaps in a forward cabin.

A feeling of deep hopelessness and dread fell over Sean. Only that same morning (or was it yesterday?) he had awakened next to his bride in the happiest and most romantic situation he could have imagined. He remembered his brief moment of concern that morning for Annie, wondering if she would adapt to life on a ranch. Now all he cared about was where she was, if she was alive, and whether she would become a widow.

"Stop this!" he said to himself in a hoarse whisper. "You've got to stay calm. Focus on how to escape. Take it one step at a time. OK, first let's learn more about this hold. It's a simple wooden box, isn't it? Any tools in here, or just the scales and slime left by thousands of previous guests."

Sean felt less anxious. His breathing became less ragged as he squirmed to move about as best he could. "Can I roll over to the other side of Cheo?" he mumbled. "Yes." But Sean paid a price: a renewed pounding at the back of his head.

"C'mon, Sean," he winced through the pain. "You've hurt worse than this. Keep looking. A knife would be nice right now. A sharp edge of any kind. Nothing? Keep looking."

Sean stopped inching as his friend's face appeared. "Whoa, Cheo. What have they done to you? I hope I don't

Kidnapped

look as bad, my friend."

Cheo's face was bruised and bloody. He had been pistol whipped to within an inch of his life. His nose was bleeding, and his eyes were swollen shut. His face was covered in caked blood. The front of his shirt was stained in crimson.

"Oh, amigo," Sean sighed. "How things would be different if only I had shot you back in Rio Bravo, taken Catharine and returned her to her chaperone or her father. Annie was on her way down here. I might be on the Rio Grande with her. Or maybe back on the Mississippi or even the Hudson. Now look what you've gotten us into.

"Yeah, I know," Sean conceded to his unconscious companion. "I could not have shot you in cold blood, even if Catharine hadn't stepped in and shielded you. I'll tell you this, my friend. I'm going to become ruthless. I'll have to be if we're to survive this one."

Sean gave one last look around the hold. His only find was Cheo's wide-brimmed hat. He gave up. There was nothing in here to help him out of his prison. Then he figured it was time to get a look at his captors.

"*¡Muchachos!*" he cried out. "*¡Por favor! ¡Tango sed! ¡Agua! ¡Por favor!*"

Would his cry for water be answered? At first, there was no sound from the deck. In a louder voice, he repeated his request. This time, his cries were answered by the sound of heavy footsteps. A man appeared above the hatch. He hunched over and peered below.

"*Hola,*" Sean said to the shadowed figure above. "*Quiero agua, por favor.*"

The man said nothing to Sean, but turned and growled to someone else that one of the captives was now awake. More conversation Sean could not translate followed, then the man unlatched the hatch and thrust a ladle through the opening.

"C'mon, fella," Sean mumbled. "Untie my hands."

River Run To Texas

Sean looked over his shoulder, uttered, "*Mis manos,*" and looked back up hopefully to the man, asking as best he could for his hands to be untied. A raspy, evil chuckle was the only answer as the man poured a bit of water from the ladle. Sean groaned and squirmed to position his head over the puddle of water. The man nodded and poured a stream onto Sean's face. He gulped what he could, then began to choke.

The man laughed but once Sean stopped coughing, he gave the man a nod and said, "*Gracias, Señor.*"

Hoping for some information on their whereabouts, he asked, "*¿A donde estamos?*" The man merely shook his head, grinning. He dropped the hatch and latched it again.

"*Señor,*" Sean said loudly. "*Mi amigo. Hace mal.*"

What's the word for hurt? he thought quickly. He tried the word for sick.

"*Mi amigo es enfermo.*"

A chorus of laughter was the only response, but it was helpful.

"Well, you can't blame a fellow for trying," Sean figured. "And I heard the voices of three men. Are you the same three who captured us in Corpus Christi? Probably."

"OK," Sean continued to himself. "Now we know a little more. We know where the latch is. We're pretty sure we're headed to Mexico by way of the Gulf, and at least three men are topside."

Sean's thoughts were interrupted by a slight stirring from Cheo. His friend moaned, and his body went rigid. His body bent as if he were trying to sit up. Then his pain produced a loud grunt and he returned to a deep unconsciousness.

Sean watched his friend with pity. "It's OK, Cheo." *Perhaps it's better for you to be out cold rather than writhing in agony.* "Unless we escape from this boat, both of us are pretty much as good as dead."

Kidnapped

Anger Gives Way To Fear

Mrs. Sean Darragh was furious. That she had no one she could direct her anger toward served only to feed her furor. As the body of the would-be abductor was removed from beside her hotel room door, Annie paced nervously back and fourth. Her husband was missing. Cheo was gone as well. Where were they?

Catharine glanced at the man slumped against the wall outside their door and quickly retreated back into the room to huddle where Annie had pulled her behind the bed. Paco brought her a glass of water and stayed at her side.

Meanwhile, small curious crowds gathered outside the courthouse and hotel as the sheriff investigated the shooting incidents. Two people were dead – one at the courthouse and one in the hotel. Gunfire was reported elsewhere. One citizen reported seeing two men with hands and feet bound, being thrown into a wagon and hauled away by three others.

"Who are these people?" Annie demanded of Catharine. Paco translated calmly back and forth, as though his soft voice might assuage Annie's temper and Catharine's grief.

"She does not recognize the man outside," Paco offered. "If he works for her father, he was hired only recently. Señorita del Carmen believes this is the work of men who knew of her father's reward for the return of the señorita and her kidnapper."

Catharine blurted a few more words, then broke into sobs

as Paco patted the young woman's hand.

"Señora Darragh," Paco said in a small voice, "Señorita del Carmen wishes you to know how sorry she is for what has happened. She feels she has caused this."

Annie sighed and knelt down beside the young girl whose entire body shook with each sob. She wrapped her arms around Catharine's and caressed her thin heaving shoulders. She was so young, so frail, so unwise in the ways of the cruel world. Then Annie said to Paco, "Remind the señorita we invited her to our wedding and tell her she is not responsible."

As Paco drew a breath, Annie interrupted, "And tell the señorita we will not lose our men. We will do everything to get them back. They *will* be safe."

Annie doubted the words, even as she spoke them, but she managed to say them with conviction; she remained strong. Tears would come to Annie; she knew they would, but not now. Not until she was alone and her anger gave way to fear.

Cleve Everline finished his conversation with the sheriff and stepped into the room. "Miss Sess ... uh, Mrs. Darragh? May I speak with you for a moment?"

Annie rose and walked to the doorway. Everline spoke in hushed tones.

"I'm sorry, but it appears Sean and Cheo were captured by these men. It looks as though they intended to abduct Catharine and Cheo and return them to Catharine's father. Sean probably wasn't their target, but he was taken as well."

"Are they alive?"

"No one knows for certain. We know two men were tied up and loaded into a wagon that left in the direction of the docks. I don't think they'd bother to tie someone who was already dead, so there is hope."

Annie bit her lip, trying to maintain her composure. "Thank you, Mr. Everline ... thank you for all you've done."

Anger Gives Way To Fear

"I'm sorry it wasn't more," he answered. "Right now, I think you, Señorita Catharine and I should decide what needs to be done next. The sheriff and the Texas Rangers have no jurisdiction south of the border. But they won't stop us from going south to rescue Sean and Cheo."

Annie looked up at Everline. "You will help us?"

"Of course," he smiled. "But we must move quickly. Every moment that passes gets them farther from us and closer to Catharine's father. Let's find a map and plot some strategy."

Everline walked over to Catharine and Paco. He started to kneel, but his legs were still too stiff from his injuries to allow it. He placed a hand on the bed to steady himself, then sat on the edge of the bed. Everline's face, hard and sinister, softened around the edges.

"Paco," he began, "there's a chance we might be able to rescue Mr. Darragh and Señor Flores. But we'll need the señorita's help. Would you ask her if she would like to help us find and rescue Sean and Cheo?"

Paco's face brightened, and he translated quickly. Catharine gasped and clasped Everline's hands. The smile through her tears and her vigorous nodding gave him his answer.

River Run To Texas

Brownsville Bound

S ean."

It came out as a half whisper, half moan with a slight gurgle at the end. Cheo had regained consciousness and called out for his friend. He hadn't moved in several hours. Now Cheo was finally awake, but his eyes were still swollen shut. He had only a general sense it was nearly dark. The hold imprisoning the two men was enveloped in shadow.

Since getting his drink, Sean had used his legs to push his companion into the shaded area of the hold where he would be cooler. Sean had also continued to think about opportunities and ways by which they might escape, but none seemed plausible if Cheo was too hurt to help. Sean spent most of his time watching the shadows to get a better sense of their direction, listening for voices and looking through the latticework of the hatch for a possible glimpse of the crew on deck. He wished he had the compass, the wedding present from the Sessions family.

"Hey, amigo," Sean whispered back. "How are you feeling?"

"*Mal. Muy mal.*"

"I'm sorry, Cheo. They must've beaten you severely. I don't know why they didn't hit me more."

"I think it was to impress Catharine's father," Cheo said. His voice was clearer now. The conversation took his mind off his aches and pains.

"Cheo, let me tell you what I know so far," Sean murmured as he inched closer to his friend. "We're on a fishing boat in the Gulf of Mexico. My guess is we're headed for the mouth of the Rio Grande or possibly farther south. There are at least three men above. One poured water on me when I asked for a drink, but the sun was in my eyes and I couldn't get a look at him to see if he was one of the men who captured us in Corpus Christi. You got all that so far?"

"What of Catharine?"

"I don't know, Cheo. I haven't heard anything to indicate she's aboard."

Cheo inhaled deeply and coughed. "We must escape."

"I know," whispered Sean, his eyes glancing anxiously toward the hatch. No one appeared. "But in order to escape, you need to recover enough to help. We need to free ourselves, but first we need some kind of plan."

"You ask for much, Sean."

"That's true, but we can't give up. Cheo, can you move your fingers?"

Cheo strained slightly against the rope that bound his hands. "Barely," came his answer.

"I can move my fingers pretty well," whispered Sean. "Let me see if I can untie you, then you can untie me. Maybe we can get a jump on these guys sometime tonight."

Both men laid on their sides, and Sean began working at the knots near Cheo's wrists.

"Sean?" Cheo said to the wooden planks in front of him.

"Yes, what?"

"This is all my fault. You should have taken Catharine back to her father. At least she'd be safe. What was I thinking? We shouldn't have come to your wedding."

"Shut up, Cheo. *Silencio, por favor,*" Sean muttered without anger. He thought a moment, then added, "You risked your life for Catharine while I was running just to save my own life. You've taught me a lot. I just wish you could teach me how to undo these knots."

"Patience, amigo. Use patience. They'll loosen in time."

An afternoon sun was winning its daily battle with the ceiling fans that tried to cool the bayfront hotel room once shared by Sean and Annie. Cleve Everline seemed most affected by the heat. He frequently swiped a handkerchief across his face as he studied a map of Mexico.

More information had come from the docks. Workers there reported seeing two men carried aboard a sloop owned by a Mexican fisherman. It set sail immediately after the men were taken below deck.

Everline was in a quandary. He had no problem with Ann Darragh going with him to attempt a rescue of Sean. She had proven time and again she was as tough as she was beautiful. Catharine del Carmen was another story. She knew the country. She knew the people, but Everline questioned whether she had the physical stamina for the pursuit of her husband's abductors. He had reservations about her emotional state as well.

"*Aquí*," she said, pointing to a spot on the map that was Los Cazaderos, her former home. Then she broke into tears. As she dabbed her eyes with a handkerchief, Everline spoke to Annie.

"The del Carmen rancho looks very accessible by river. My guess is they will sail to Matamoros, then switch to a riverboat for the rest of the trip. Either that or go by road."

"Could they come into the Mexican coast farther south and go inland from there?" asked Annie.

Paco interrupted and answered for Catharine. "It is not likely. A long finger of land goes south many miles. They would have to sail around it, then go ashore, probably to the village of Carboneras. Roads go only north and south from there. They would have to take a road back to Matamoros. It would add two or three days to their trip for nothing."

"OK," answered Everline. "First, I will send a telegram to Dudley Latham in Brownsville, asking him to watch for the sloop. Mr. Latham and his men may be able to intercept it and rescue Sean and Cheo. In the meantime, we need to get to Brownsville as quickly as possible. I will inquire downstairs and at the telegraph office as to the fastest way. Any other suggestions?"

Four people looked at one another, each hoping the other would come up with the answer. Paco provided it: "A boat, Señor. There is a road to Brownsville, but travel is slow, with frequent stops for water."

"Then boat it is," Everline nodded. "Mrs. Darragh, let's you and I go send our wire, then on to the port to see if we can arrange transportation."

Catharine picked up on Paco's expression of concern, and both asked the question, "What about us?" One in Spanish and one in English. Everline quickly reviewed the situation. If Latham's net failed to snag the boat that carried Sean and Cheo, Catharine and Paco's knowledge would be essential. With a long sigh, Everline announced his consent.

"You come with us," he said as he beckoned with his long, bony fingers. "But understand, Paco, we may have to leave the señorita if she is unable to keep up."

Paco nodded and translated for Catharine. As she beamed her gratitude, Paco offered, "Señor Everline, I will pack your bags, then meet you at the docks. We will also bring extra food and water."

"You are mature far beyond your years, Paco," answered Everline. "OK, we'll meet you on the docks. Let's get moving."

The telegraph office was small, hot and dusty. Only two people worked in the office, a grim-faced woman at the counter and a bespectacled telegrapher hunched over his key.

Several couriers and others waited in a line to send their wires. Everline sweated profusely as he waited impatiently. Annie, sensing time was slipping away, spoke up.

"Mr. Everline, why don't I go ahead to the port? I know enough about the business that I can at least begin the process of finding us transportation."

"I hate for you to go alone to those docks," replied Everline. "It's no place for a lady."

"I can take care of myself. You know that. Paco and Catharine might beat us there if I wait with you. Yes, sir, I've made up my mind. You send the telegram, and I'll find us a charter to Brownsville."

Everline looked down at the determined young woman and smiled. "Find us a good one, Annie."

The *Cyrus Fishborne*

*T*he sun had already disappeared behind a huge bank of clouds on the horizon when Annie reached the docks of the port at Corpus Christi. She shivered and wrapped her shawl tighter as she searched for an office where she might charter a boat.

She came upon a small wooden building, weathered from hard rains and strong wind. The warm glow of a lantern drew her inside. The balding, heavyset man was sifting through stacks of paperwork, obviously disgruntled at his job. He frowned as he looked up from his papers. He did not rise to his feet.

"What do you want here? I'm very busy."

Ignoring his abrupt manner, Annie shot back, "I have an extreme emergency and need a fast boat that can carry four passengers to Brownsville."

The man shook his head. "We've got no boats going to Brownsville."

Annie clenched her fists, her face tense and determined. As she turned to leave, the man said in a softer voice, "Miss, I think a steamboat owned by Cyrus Fishborne may be leaving for Brownsville later this evening. It's two piers to the east."

Annie wheeled around, "Oh, thank you, sir. That's wonderful news. And the name of the boat?"

"The *Cyrus Fishborne*, of course," he answered with a shrug.

119

River Run To Texas

Annie hurried down the docks as fast as she could in the darkening light. She gasped. Yes, it was the *Cyrus Fishborne.* She was nearly new! Despite a strong breeze, the air was filled with the smells of varnish and paint from her deckworks. She was, perhaps, 160 feet, a side-wheeler, but she also was fitted with spars for running with the wind. Several men were carrying firewood from the dock up her gangplank.

"Hello the *Cyrus Fishborne,*" Annie called out to the men aboard. "Is the captain aboard?"

Two men looked with amusement at a third. He was very young and very tall with long hair that nearly touched his broad shoulders. He wore no shirt but quickly snatched one up and pulled it on as he answered, "Madam, you're looking at the captain. Cyrus Fishborne, at your service."

Annie gulped. "Sir, may I come aboard? I wish to charter your vessel immediately."

Finding work was not supposed to be this easy or this pleasant, Fishborne said to himself as he motioned the young woman aboard. But after a few moments of conversation with Annie, young Fishborne called out to his crew, "Make ready to sail. We leave for Brownsville within the hour."

The fishing boat that carried Cheo and Sean toward Mexico was now well off the coast. A quarter moon was the only source of light. There was no light for the prisoners, but Sean believed that worked to their advantage since it would be hard to spot the two men working feverishly to free themselves.

Sean's fingers were puckered, wet and numb. Most of his fingernails were cracked from fumbling, pulling and pinching in an effort to loosen the knots binding Cheo's hands. Finally, a break. The boat rode up a high swell, then crashed into the trough. Water poured into the smelly, grimy hold that was their prison. The water was salty and soaked the two men, but it also soaked the ropes. Sean continued to work one spot back and forth. A knot that once seemed like cement quickly softened and gave way to Sean's tugging.

"Bully," Sean whispered excitedly. "I'm making some progress now."

No response came from Cheo who had passed out. It took Sean another 10 minutes to free Cheo. As he pulled the ropes away, Cheo's hands fell limp, still behind his back. Sean nudged Cheo. No response. He nudged harder, and Cheo groaned.

"Cheo, wake up," Sean said coarsely. "You've got to wake up, man. Your hands are free."

Slowly, Cheo began to regain consciousness. If anything, he felt worse than before. Now, in addition to his injuries, he was seasick.

"I feel terrible."

"Come on, Cheo, we're going to capture this boat and find Catharine and Annie. Don't fail me now. You can get through this."

Cheo wasn't so sure, but he moved his stiff and aching arms to strain against the ropes. To his surprise, his hands were free. He rubbed them together vigorously and was rewarded with a tingling in his fingers. In just a few moments, he had full use of his hands. Cheo still felt nauseous, and he could barely see through puffy eyes. Still, he managed a slight grin of victory as he whispered, "Roll over, Sean, and I'll untie you."

Free at last, Sean crawled to the edge of the hatch. He could see nothing, but he stuck his fingers through the latticework. Poking around, he determined the position of the latch. He couldn't reach the clasp with his fingers, but he remembered how easily it had come open for the man who had given him water. From his experience on other boats, he was sure a mere twist of the clasp would unlock the latch.

He crawled back to his companion and announced excitedly, "Cheo, if we can come up with a few inches of wire, I think we can get out of here."

Cheo squinted through swollen eyelids. "Is *that* all you need?" He grabbed his hat and twisted the brim back and forth. There was a soft *snap*, and he pulled a long wire from the edge of the brim. Then he handed it to Sean with a half grimace, half grin. "Anything else?"

Sean shook his head, stifling a laugh, and crawled back to the latch. He bent a hook into one end of the wire and began fishing about the clasp. It took dozens of tries and several modifications of bends in the wire, but as the small boat kept doggedly pushing toward the Rio Grande, Sean finally pulled the clasp free. One good push and the hatch would open.

"Cheo, are you able to fight?" asked Sean.

"But of course," he answered. "Do you have a plan?"

"Yes, but not much of one," admitted Sean. "Let's put our heads together."

It was dark now. So dark that Cleve Everline would not know where the Gulf's water ended and the heavens began were it not for the billions of stars that filled the night sky. Water gurgled incessantly under the *Cyrus Fishborne's* bow, but even the wake was too dark to see. Everline glanced back to the boat's twin stacks and shuddered.

"Are you cold, Mr. Everline?" asked Cyrus Fishborne.

"No, not really," answered the detective. "Just an old injury acting up."

Annie said nothing but correctly assumed Everline was wrestling with the demons that had haunted him since he was nearly killed in the explosion of a riverboat on the Mississippi. He was nervous even with the leisurely pace of the large steamboats that had carried Annie and him to Texas to find Sean. Annie had noticed it, and he admitted then he felt a bit jumpy on the deck of a steamboat.

"Mr. Fishborne," she began, "how old is your boat?"

"Her hull was launched eight months ago in Pittsburgh. Her deckworks were completed in Chesapeake Bay only six weeks ago, and the trip around the Keys to New Orleans was her maiden voyage. I plan to carry freight and passengers between New Orleans, Indianola and Brownsville. That's why I was headed to Brownsville when you came along."

"She's a fine boat," complimented Annie. "But as much as we want to reach Brownsville quickly, I don't want you putting too much stress on her boilers."

"Don't worry, Mrs. Darragh," laughed Fishborne. "She's put me too far in debt to send her to the bottom and me to the devil. No, we're only at 75 percent capacity now, and she's making a good 20 knots. Well, maybe 18. But we're light. Very little cargo. Depending on the winds and the sailboat we're chasing, we might even catch up with them just before we reach Port Isabel."

Fishborne couldn't see it, but his words comforted both Annie and Everline. They both broke into broad smiles. Annie tried in vain to scan the darkness, wishing to see the boat that carried her new husband. Knowing it was out there filled her heart at once with both fear and hope.

Escape

*D*awn was still an hour away from Brownsville, Texas. A startled cat hissed and leapt into the bushes as Richard Glassford approached the livery stable where four horses belonging to D. Latham & Co. were stabled. He grabbed a saddle and quickly readied a horse to ride.

Glassford was one of Latham's first hires, but he was far from the best. He was young, strong and spoke some Spanish. A native of the area, he knew many people on both sides of the Rio Grande. This made him a valuable employee, but Glassford's problem stemmed from his attitude. He wanted wealth and all its trappings, but lacked the ambition and drive to achieve it.

Yesterday, he stumbled onto an opportunity to change all that.

"Morning, Dick."

The greeting came from Glassford's friend, Wally Nicholson. He was a mechanic for Latham.

"Hullo, Wally. You headed for the *James H. Dawkins*?"

"Yup, thought I'd run her out to Port Isabel. Need to make sure she's running all right, don'tcha know."

"Fancy that," chuckled Glassford. "I'm on my way to the lighthouse to be on the lookout for the boat that may carry Darragh and his friend." Then he added in a low voice, "You watch the lighthouse. I'll signal you if I see anything, then I'll be down to the boat as fast as I can make it."

Cheo Flores was hurting. His head ached, his bruises tender and sore. His limbs alternated between numbness and cramping. Nausea from the seasickness came and went with effort. Yet he was ready, even anxious, to overpower their captors. Better to die in a fight than to go on feeling this miserable, he reasoned.

The Gulf was still cloaked in black ink. Sean was grateful for it. The odds were against Sean and Cheo, but the blackness would provide some measure of cover as they attempted their escape. Gunmen could not easily hit their targets in the cover of night.

Sean and Cheo assumed there would be one person at the helm and two or three asleep elsewhere, probably the cabin. The breeze that was strong earlier in the night had dwindled. Winds were light now, and the boat seemed to bob and pitch more than plow ahead. Every now and then, Sean could feel the hull respond to the sculling of the rudder, a maneuver to keep the boat moving ahead and on course.

"I'll take the pilot," said Sean. "You go forward and take the guys sleeping. Once I've subdued the guy at the helm, I'll come forward to help you."

"Hurry forward, Sean," answered Cheo. "I am not at my best right now."

"You'll do fine." Sean felt admiration for his friend. "I know you'll do fine. I remember all too well your ability to ambush and subdue your adversaries."

Cheo felt apologetic, but managed a slight grin through his puffy lips. "An old Army pistol would be good now."

"I don't know what we'll find in the way of clubs or weapons," continued Sean. "Let's attack first and worry about weapons later. You ready?"

Escape

"I'm ready. Let's do it."

As best they could, Sean and Cheo stretched their arms and legs several times, then moved near the latch. Sean pushed gently on the hatch. It didn't budge. He tried rocking it slightly. Still no luck. To his companion, he whispered, "It's still stuck a bit. I've got to break it. There's going to be some noise."

Sean moved to a squatting position. He held his arms out to his side, flexed his legs a couple of times, then raised up quickly with a grunt, hitting the hatch hard with his back. The latch popped free, and the hatch flew up.

Moving quickly, Sean crouched a second time and jumped up. Aching arms went down. He grabbed the rail of the hold. He threw himself onto the deck and scrambled to his feet. He could hear Cheo struggling to clear the hold. Sean lurched and stumbled the few feet back toward the stern.

A large figure appeared and yelled. Sean was upon him before he drew another breath to yell again. Sean drove his head into the pilot's midsection and knocked the man back. He heard a huge whoosh of air. The pilot began kicking wildly as he held his stomach, struggling to breathe.

Cheo stumbled forward. He found a hammock stretched from the edge of the cabin to the rail. Its occupant raised up but was off balance in the sling. With a guttural, animal-like sound, Cheo squatted, scooped up the hammock with the man struggling inside it, and in one quick motion, threw the man overboard. The man let out a scream, then another. His third was cut off as he sank below the surface.

Back at the stern, Sean's victim gasped for air. Sean looked about quickly. There was nothing to use as a club. Grabbing the man's long hair, he beat his head against the deck once, twice, a third time. The man still struggled. Sean grabbed him once more and threw him against the deck even harder. The man's body sagged and was still.

Sean looked about again. Still no weapon. No pistol on the

pilot. He heard Cheo's roar and the screams that followed. As he searched about, Sean saw the face of his victim. He was an old man, old enough to be Sean's father. He was shocked. The remorse couldn't be helped, but Sean put it aside. He was fighting for his life. Age didn't matter.

Cheo rushed madly about the deck, bumping into everything, groaning curses in his native tongue. Then he heard scuffling inside the cabin. He felt his way to the cabin hatch. Men inside were yelling to the pilot. One popped out of the hatch to the cabin. Cheo grabbed at his gun. He caught the man's wrist instead and pulled him out of the opening and onto the deck.

Sean rushed forward. Cheo was on top of his man but could do nothing more than keep the man pinned down. Sean flung himself at the gun. The man squeezed it tightly, but the hammer was down. It couldn't fire. Sean bit the man's hand, hard, until he tasted blood. The man screamed but held fast. Cheo began slugging the man as fast and as hard as he could. Finally, the gun fell loose.

As Sean grabbed it, he heard yet another man yell, then fire his pistol. The slug splintered the boom just above Cheo's head. Sean rolled away and fumbled at the other pistol, pulling the hammer back. The man moved closer to Cheo. There was just enough light for Sean to see the figure pointing his gun to fire again. Sean's pistol roared. The shadowy figure fell with a thud and lay silent.

"Throw them in the hold!" yelled Sean. He stuffed his pistol in his belt and grabbed the ankles of the man he shot. He struggled to get him to the hold.

Cheo's voice rose above Sean's grunts, "Sean, he is dead."

Sean froze. He was panting, gasping, trying to hold back the rising bile. Cheo called out, "Help me with this one."

They pulled the pilot and Cheo's second victim into the hold and secured the hatch. The boat bobbed aimlessly. They searched the boat until they were satisfied no one else was on board. They found a bucket of drinking water and some dried fish, their first food since breakfast nearly 24 hours ago. As the eastern sky slowly lightened from black to gray, Sean steered the boat back to a southwesterly direction, then tied the helm as Cheo adjusted the sail for a close reach. The two men collapsed exhausted on the deck.

"This is one of the men who cornered us," Cheo muttered as he studied the face of the gunshot victim.

Sean ignored Cheo's chatter. He was inspecting the footwell just forward of the helm.

"Cheo, this boat is taking on water." Sean sprang to his feet and disappeared into the cabin. A moment later, he emerged carrying a can. "We need to start bailing if we're going to stay afloat. There must be 3 feet of water below the floor."

"Bailing?" Cheo asked, not understanding the word or the seriousness of their situation.

"The boat is leaking," Sean explained. "Water is collecting inside. If we don't collect it and throw it out, we'll sink before we can make land."

Sean began to bail with the can. Cheo found a canvas bucket and did the same. After a few minutes, Cheo asked, "Are we making any progress?"

"Hard to tell," answered Sean. "We've got to keep bailing though. If we can just keep up with the amount of water that's leaking into the boat, we'll be all right."

To the east, the sun rose behind a bank of clouds and a fresh breeze blew once more. After nearly an hour of bailing, they were fighting a losing battle. Then they heard the cries from the hold. They had forgotten their prisoners. Cheo went forward and talked to the men through the hatch.

"Sean, the hold is filling with water. Our prisoners ask if they can help bail. The old one says the boat is his, and that it will surely sink unless they bail as well."

"One of us will have to guard them if we let them out," warned Sean.

"I'll keep a pistol on them," promised Cheo.

"OK, let them bail the hold while you watch them."

Three men bailed furiously, but it made no difference. Each time they scooped up water and threw it overboard, even more water rushed in. The hold where the two prisoners worked was taking on even more water. Then, peering through the haze, Cheo spotted land.

"Sean! Sean! I see land! Land is ahead to the right!"

Sean leaped to the top of the cabin for a look. "Yes!" he exclaimed. "We'll alter course and head for it."

A few minutes later, the boat was on a broad reach, headed due west toward sandy dunes. Not long after the new course was set, Cheo yelled, "Sean! Off to the left! I see smoke."

Again, Sean interrupted his bailing to stare. "It's a steamboat," he said. "But we have no way of indicating we're in trouble. Let's continue our course toward land."

The steamboat continued to close in on the small fishing sloop, even as it slogged toward land. Sean kept interrupting his bailing to squint into the distance at the boat. As it drew closer and closer, Sean noted familiar features. At first he dismissed any notion he might know the vessel. But as it bore down on the sloop, and before he could read the name on the bow, he realized he knew the boat. Knew it well, in fact.

"Cheo, I do believe we're rescued. That steamboat is coming for us, and we both know her well. It's the *James H. Dawkins!*"

Escape

Betrayed

Sean's old friend, the *James H. Dawkins*, made a graceful turn into the wind, and her paddles slowed enough to keep her hovering in the shallow gulf water. The prisoners aboard the sloop continued to bail, but Sean steered the boat alongside the *Dawkins* and let its sails luff. Standing at the steamboat's rail, Wally Nicholson tossed Sean a line.

"We thought we were going to have to shoot up your boat to rescue you," called Nicholson. "Looks like you turned the tables somewhere along the way."

"We got lucky," chuckled Sean as he tied the sloop fast to the *Dawkins'* rail. Cheo slipped over the rail and stuck his pistol into his belt. "How'd you know we were here?" Sean asked.

"Your friend Everline wired Latham the sloop might be headed for the Rio Grande. Your bride, Everline and your buddy's girlfriend are on their way down here. Latham was still on his way from Corpus Christi when the wire came, but Glassford got it and spotted you from the Port Isabel lighthouse."

The news astonished Sean. "We're that close?"

"Less than a mile away," Nicholson affirmed. Then he saw the prisoners in the hold. "Want us to shoot those Mexicans for you?"

Sean glared at Nicholson, "No, Wally. I don't. One of them is an old man whose only mistake was to carry the wrong cargo. The other is no threat to us now. We'll just let them have their ..."

Sean's words were cut off by gunfire. The younger prisoner screamed in pain and fell into the hold. The old man took cover inside the hold as well. Sean couldn't believe his eyes. He swung around and looked up. The smoke still curled from the barrel of Glassford's rifle. He was calmly reloading as Sean screamed, "Glassford! Put down your arms!"

Cheo whipped out his pistol, but Nicholson already had his gun aimed at Cheo's breast. "Drop it, Flores, or I'll put a slug through your chest."

Cheo quickly considered his options. Both men were armed. He could shoot Nicholson, but he'd likely be hit in return fire from Nicholson or Glassford. Sean was unarmed. It was useless. He bent over slightly and dropped the pistol to the deck. Sean was still in shock. "What th–" he muttered to no one in particular.

"Sean, you just got unlucky again," sneered Nicholson.

As Glassford came down from the pilothouse, Nicholson explained, "Your bandit friend here is worth a lot of money. His girlfriend's daddy has offered a big reward, and we figure there might be a bonus if we also hand over the guy who let the bandit keep his daughter in the first place."

Sean broke in. "So you didn't come out here to rescue us. You just wanted to kill our abductors and deliver us to Señor del Carmen yourselves."

"That's right." It was Glassford. He walked up holding a pistol on Sean and Cheo. He began to work at a line wrapped around a rail cleat.

"And Dud never got Everline's telegram," continued Sean.

"Right again," Glassford said as he untied the line that secured the sloop and tossed it overboard. The sloop slowly drifted away as the old man cowered in the hold with his injured companion. "As far as Latham knows, you're on your honeymoon. Wally, bring the irons. We'll put them in the cargo hold."

Sean and Cheo's new prison was a cargo bay. It was large and it didn't smell like the sloop's hold, but escape was out of the question. They were shackled together, sitting with their backs to opposite sides of a post that ran floor to ceiling.

Wally Nicholson returned to the engine room and stoked the boilers. Richard Glassford climbed back up to the pilothouse and signaled for three-quarters speed. The *James H. Dawkins* belched new smoke, and her paddles slapped harder as she turned toward Port Isabel. This was going to be easy money.

Cyrus Fishborne held a glass to one eye as his namesake boat surged ahead. His passengers had given way to exhaustion and were asleep in their quarters. Even with the telescope, Fishborne could barely make out the puff of smoke in the distance. Another steamboat, he reasoned, but it was a sloop they were after. He checked his watch. A quarter past 8. He figured their position to be only about half an hour from Brazos Santiago.

"Time to wake up our passengers," Fishborne told his first mate. "They'll want to be ready to move out as soon as we make port. Drat, I wish we could have overtaken that sloop."

The mate quickly descended the ladder from the pilothouse and began knocking on cabin doors. A few minutes later, Fishborne observed he could now see, without the telescope, the smoke trailing from the steamboat he noticed earlier. He tied off his wheel and put the telescope to his eye once more.

This time, he could see the boat through the glass. He

watched it for a moment, then panned back along the shoreline. A tiny, white triangle of sail caught his eye. *Could it be?* Fishborne quickly compacted the scope, placed it in its holder, slipped the loop from the wheel and began turning the boat to starboard. His mate returned and noticed the turn.

"What's happening, sir?" he asked.

"I saw a sail," he replied, not taking his eye from the spot. "It could be the sloop we're after."

"We need to watch out for shallow water," reminded the mate.

"I know, we're only going in about a mile for a closer look. Just in case, ready the launch."

A mile later, Fishborne signaled to cut all speed and again pulled the scope out. It was a sloop grounded a few hundred yards from the beach. He saw one man in the boat, a man waving his arms – a distress signal.

Fishborne asked for a depth reading and turned the helm over to his mate. He hurried down to Annie's cabin and knocked. Annie's face appeared at the door. Fishborne took off his cap. "Mrs. Darragh, we've spotted a small sailboat in distress. We can't tell if it's the one we're after, but we can send in the launch to investigate, or continue to Brazos Santiago. That's about 20 minutes away."

"If you feel it's best to send the launch, then do," said Annie. "But if this is the wrong boat, I hope your men will return quickly once they've made their rescue."

"I'll so order it," Fishborne said as he replaced his cap. "We'll send the mate and two crewmen. One speaks Spanish, and all are good with weapons."

The launch was rowed to the sloop. It quickly returned with two men. One was wounded. As the men came aboard, the first mate reported to Fishborne and Annie's party.

"It was the right boat," exclaimed the mate. "But the two men you seek are no longer aboard. They were taken prisoners by men aboard the steamboat."

"They're lying," cried Annie. "That doesn't make sense."

"Ma'am, with all due respect, I think they're telling the truth," said the mate. "We searched the sloop thoroughly, and they're not aboard. They had no reason to tell us about your husband and his friend. In fact, they would have been better off to lie and say they knew nothing about him."

Annie could only agree with the mate's assessment, but that did nothing to assuage her grief. She turned to Everline and wept bitter tears. Catharine knelt beside the two Mexicans and began asking more questions. In a few moments, she rose and said to Fishborne, "We must go ... Matamoros. Fast. ¡Ahora!"

There was a moment of silence as Annie, Everline and Fishborne looked at one another. Then, turning to his crew, Fishborne said, "You heard the señorita. Let's move!"

The River Race

With a slight nod and *"Gracias,"* Catharine del Carmen took the pen from Cyrus Fishborne and poised it above the map. Starting at Matamoros, she drew a line almost due west, making a slight turn at one spot. She spoke softly as the ink dried.

Paco translated for her: "The journey to her rancho is faster by horseback than by boat. She says this trail south of the Rio Grande is not well known but has been used by her father many times when he goes to Matamoros. There is a small village called Tampita where fresh horses can be obtained."

Paco paused and listened to Catharine, his eyes searching her face in disbelief. She stopped speaking, but Paco remained silent.

"Di les," she commanded Paco to "tell them."

"The señorita has decided the only way Cheo and Señor Darragh can be saved is for us to reach her father before they do," Paco said, his eyes darting between Catharine and those around the captain's desk. "She believes if we take the same route along the river, we cannot overtake them."

"The lady has a point," agreed Everline. "It would take us at least two hours to transfer from this ship to a steamboat. We can't catch them by boat."

Annie was full of doubt. "But even if we do get to Catharine's father before they do, he might kill us all, then kill Sean and Cheo. Besides, how will we get horses? How can we be sure of the fresh horses?"

Paco was translating for Catharine when she suddenly broke in, "¡No! *Mi papa* no kill! No kill!" Her eyes narrowed as she glared at Annie.

Paco followed up: "Señorita says her father believes she was taken against her will. She believes she may be able to ... to calm her father." Paco looked at Catharine in clear anguish. Instinctively, like a brother, he put his skinny arm around the young woman's shoulder. "Señorita believes the worse that will happen is her father will send Cheo away, and she will become a prisoner in her home. She doesn't believe her father will harm anyone."

"This is ridiculous," said Annie. "We can get a faster boat and overtake them."

"No, we *can't*, Annie," interrupted Everline. "I've learned that the hard way."

"¡*Pantalones!*" Catharine cried in a strong voice. She slapped at her thighs. Then she rushed from the door of the captain's cabin.

Paco looked about the adults around him, then translated, "Pants, Señora Darragh. You'll need to wear pants for the ride."

Sean Darragh could tell the way the engine slowed that the *James H. Dawkins* was most likely navigating past Brownsville and Matamoros. Sean thought of yelling, but he knew his voice would barely be heard aboard the steamboat. There was no way his voice could carry to a passing boat or to someone on shore.

"You OK, Cheo?" he asked.

"Still tired and sore, amigo, but I'll be OK."

"You know, the boat won't be able to make it all the way to

Mexico," reasoned Sean. "That means we'll probably go the rest of the way on horseback or in a wagon."

"That's what I figure. What are you thinking?"

"Maybe that will give us a chance for escape," Sean said hopefully.

"Perhaps, but I fear your friends are more careful than the others."

"They're no friends, but you're right, Cheo, they are smarter. I think I'll try to sleep, if that's possible. Something tells me we're going to need as much strength as we can muster."

Cheo didn't answer. He stared at the cargo bay bulkheads, but his mind was on his Catharine. He wondered if she also was a captive. If so, was she being treated well? Was she terrified? He shut his eyes tightly to fight back the fears. He remembered when Sean burst into their room and leveled a gun at him, Catharine had rushed in between them. *No*, he thought, *Catharine is not terrified. Scared, maybe, but not to the point of losing control.* She had shown herself to be a strong and courageous young woman. And right now, Cheo loved her so much his heart ached more than his bruises.

Cyrus Fishborne's mate gave one more stroke with his oars, and the launch surged toward the dock at Matamoros. Annie reached out and caught the dock. Then she tossed the bowline to a helper while Fishborne did the same at the stern. First out of the launch were Catharine and Paco.

"Wait here!" Paco cried as he scrambled to keep up with the señorita. "We will return with the horses." They ran to a horse-drawn buggy, spoke quickly to the driver, then hopped aboard. The buggy disappeared in a cloud of dust.

Annie looked at Everline with exasperation but said nothing. Dressed in borrowed pants, she felt foolish and out of place. Fishborne and his first mate waited with Annie and Everline. Annie paced the dock for half an hour, her hopes of rescuing her husband fading fast.

"Catharine could have been captured, you know," she blurted, casting an accusatory glance toward Everline.

"Give them another half hour," Everline replied as he studied the watch pulled from his vest. "I can see if a riverboat is ..." Everline sprang to his feet as four horses clattered up to the dock.

"¡Hola!" sang out Catharine as she slipped effortlessly from the saddle. Her dark hair was pulled back into a ponytail. A straw sombrero rode on her shoulders, held by a leather strap. She untied another hat from the saddlebag and tucked it under her arm as she skipped up to Annie. She took Annie by the shoulders, turned her around and whipped out a bandanna, which she tied neatly on Annie's head. As Catharine tied the bandanna, Paco provided the instructions.

"You will be more comfortable with a hat," he said. "On the side of each saddle, you will find a *bota* filled with water. Do not drink too much, too fast. Señorita del Carmen will take the lead."

Addressing both Annie and Everline, he continued. "You will not need to direct your ponies. They will follow the señorita's horse. I will ride in back. Do not let your pony run. We will ride at a gallop. Hold the *pomo* with one hand until you are used to riding. We must mount now and be on our way. We will have fresh horses in six hours' time."

Paco gave Annie the reins and helped guide her left foot to the stirrup. Putting decorum aside, he squatted, placed both hands on Annie's bottom and boosted her up into the saddle as Catharine held the pony by the strap near its ear. Everline mounted with only a little difficulty. Catharine and Paco flung themselves into their saddles. Catharine pulled her reins to one side and spurred her mount. Annie nearly lost her grip and fell backward as her pony jerked into motion. Fishborne yelled, "Goodbye and good luck," but Annie was too focused on trying to keep astride her pony to even attempt a wave.

Adobe buildings slipped by as the horses loped down the narrow streets of Matamoros. As they reached the edge of town, Catharine again dug her spurs into her mare's flanks, and Paco gave a short, shrill whistle. In unison, the four animals broke into a gallop. The trail narrowed as buildings gave way to cholla, ironwood and an occasional juniper.

Annie had said nothing back in Matamoros, but this was only the third time in her young life she had been astride a horse and the first time didn't count. It came when she was 9 years old as her grandfather led her around a corral. She glanced back at Everline. He managed a grin, but he seemed equally out of place in his suit and bowler hat.

No matter. They were headed west into the morning sun across hot, dry country.

"Sean, you had better make it to where we're going," she said aloud to her absent husband. "I'm not leaving this country without you."

Overland Chase

*T*he day had begun hot, but now with the sun high and blazing, the Mexican countryside had become a furnace. A wisp of southerly breeze helped evaporate the sweat, but Cleve Everline could have used more. The trail widened as it meandered around small hills dotted with desert vegetation. The ponies, lathered in foamy sweat, were at a walk now, and Paco had pulled his mount abreast of Everline. It gave the detective time to ask questions he had pondered for several hours.

"How did you manage to get these horses, Paco?"

"Señorita del Carmen went to a stable where her father trades. The owner is very old, very nice. He loaned us the horses, saddles, everything. He was happy to find the señorita safe."

Everline watched a lizard scurry across a large flat rock and wondered how this harsh and unforgiving land could be labeled as safe, especially for a woman.

Just in front of Everline, Annie was in pain. With every bounce, she hurt – from her ankles rubbed by the stirrups to a persistent pain in her side. Her seat and thighs seemed to burn. She had given up trying to copy Catharine's erect, yet graceful style in the saddle. Now, Annie rode bent over, her shoulders slumped. Her spirit slumped as well.

"There is no way we can beat them to Catharine's rancho," she bleated to no one in particular.

Paco translated Annie's cry, and Catharine responded in a strong, clear voice.

"The señorita estimates we are at least as far west as the steamboat," announced Paco. "And, of course, we are already as far south as the rancho. We will easily beat them there."

Catharine pointed toward a windmill turning lazily in the breeze. "*Agua*," she cried as she spurred her horse. About a hundred yards later, she slowed her pony to a walk. The mare picked her way carefully over sharp rocks, her ears pricked forward. As she picked up the scent of water, she leapt over several large rocks. The other ponies followed her lead, and Annie dropped the reins and held the pommel tightly. She was almost in tears as the horses gathered around a wooden trough. As they sucked the water greedily, Annie tried to dismount. Her legs felt like rubber; they began to tremble. Paco helped her down.

"I can't go on," she moaned. "I don't think I can even get back on my horse."

Paco spoke briefly with Catharine who turned and pulled a towel from her saddlebag. She gave it to Annie as she patted her arm, and Paco provided the instructions.

"Señorita del Carmen will help you put this in your pants," he said to the ground, too embarrassed to look Annie in the eye. "Behind that bush would be good. Don't worry, Señora Darragh, the worst is behind us. Fresh horses are less than five miles away, and we can rest again as the saddles are changed."

The words were of little comfort to Annie, but she followed Catharine obediently. When she reappeared, the seat of her pants looked a bustle. Everline tried in vain to suppress a laugh.

"Annie, if it helps, I'm hurting, too," he chuckled.

"It doesn't help," she replied curtly.

As Paco raised the stirrups on Annie's saddle, he advised,

"Now you can stand on your stirrups to relieve the pressure on ... you."

"*Adelante*," Catharine ordered, and the foursome mounted once more and continued their ride west at a trot.

About 20 miles to the northeast, the *James H. Dawkins* was lodged in the silt of the Rio Grande. The river was no longer deep enough to accommodate the steamer. Glassford and his engineer saddled four horses in stalls aboard the boat and led them off the gangplank to a stand of ironwood trees. They tied the horses, then returned for their captives. As Glassford held a gun on Sean and Cheo, Nicholson tied their hands.

"Don't try anything," warned Glassford. "You're worth as much dead as alive, and you'd be far less trouble stretched over your saddles."

"You may turn us over to the Mexicans, but you'll never get the money," muttered Sean. "If they kill us, they'll kill you as well."

"I don't think so," replied Glassford. "Señor del Carmen is a man of honor."

"What do you know of honor?" Cheo shot back.

Glassford ignored the remark as Nicholson nudged Sean and Cheo with his gun barrel, forcing them to their feet. One at a time, they were led down the gangplank to the waiting horses. Nicholson hooked their arms over the pommels, guided their boots into stirrups and boosted them into the saddles. Then he tied a length of rope binding their wrists to each pommel.

"We'd better skirt Rio Bravo," Glassford said to Nicholson. "I figure about five or six hours to the rancho. Let's get moving."

As the two men and their captives rode to the southwest, Paco was cinching the fourth saddle of the pursuers in a corral at Tampita.

"All set," he said happily.

Catharine clasped the hands of the horses' owner and smiled. *"Muchas gracias."*

"Bueno suerte," he smiled back. *"Vaya con Dios."*

Annie's hope had returned. She put aside her pain and mounted without assistance. She, too, waved a thank-you to the owner and followed Catharine from the corral. This time, she had no trouble staying glued to the saddle as her horse broke into a lope.

As they galloped west, Annie realized she had misjudged Catharine. There was far more depth to this shy, beautiful girl than Annie had first thought. For the first time, she trusted Catharine. She believed in her and her plan to reach the rancho first.

Would Sean make it to the rancho alive? Was Catharine right about her father's ability to forgive his daughter's actions?

Annie was soon to find out.

Overland Chase

Los Cazaderos

*F*our horses clattered single file over rock and caliche in a steady walk. No need to rush, Glassford figured. He knew in general where he was going, but he didn't know the whereabouts of watering holes. The horses had to last the journey. They also needed strength in case of a surprise attack by bandits.

Glassford took the lead, leading Sean, whose mount was tied to Cheo's. Nicholson took the rear. His rifle rested in the scabbard on the left side of his saddle. Glassford carried his rifle in the same manner.

Cheo soon realized that with constant effort, he would be able to free his hands, but their captors had forbidden him to even look at Sean. He tested the order once and was rewarded with a slash across his face from Glassford's quirt. It was a single whip blow, but enough to open a wound from the beating at the hands of his first Mexican captors.

Sean worked at his bonds as well but with no success. Like his bride of three days, he also suffered the aches and pains that came with being too long in the saddle. He had ridden horses a few times since coming to Texas but never for this long.

How long have we been riding? At least three, maybe four hours, with only two stops to rest. Or so it seemed.

He figured they would reach Catharine's rancho by sundown. What would happen then? He could only guess.

Although the heat was unbearable, he shuddered thinking he might die without seeing Annie again.

Thoughts of her kept him from giving up. He pictured her aboard the *Drake*, the moonlight captured by her deep blue eyes. He could almost smell her sweet fragrance.

Thank goodness Annie could handle a gaff or he might have been engulfed by the swirling waters of the Hudson. As it was, he drowned in her lovely gaze the moment he saw her.

When he told her he was leaving the *Drake* for a life in Texas, he thought he'd lost her forever. But it was Annie who rescued him from Everline's grasp and begged him to flee.

Sean remembered the joy of seeing her step from the cabin of the scow at Codo del Diablo. Everline clearing his name was a relief, but hearing Annie offer him one more chance was a godsend.

If only she would suddenly appear now ... if only!

At that moment, Annie rode just behind Catharine. Paco and Everline followed. Annie had learned to give her pony plenty of rein as he stepped gingerly over rocks in a trail leading up from an arroyo and up a large hill. As they reached the ridge, all four steeds stopped abreast of each other. There in the distance, less than a mile atop another swell, lay the rambling estate fortress.

As Catharine scanned the landscape, emotions of first joy, then satisfaction fleetingly touched her face. Fear remained. She spoke but two words – *"Los Cazaderos."*

"What now?" Everline asked, breaking the silence. "Does Catharine ride in alone or all of us together?

His answer came from an outcrop of boulders to the right along the ridgeline.

"¡Alto!"

Catharine wheeled her mare quickly toward the sound. The other horses spooked, then wheeled, testing their riders' strength. Two horsemen had rifles drawn, their sights trained on the group. Everline instinctively pulled his pistol in defense.

A shot! Everline twisted and fell from his horse.

"No!" Annie screamed.

Catharine and Paco yelled angrily in Spanish. The men rode up, their guns now challenging the rest of the riders. Everline writhed in pain in the shade of his horse's belly.

Annie didn't care about their guns. Her friend was in trouble. She rushed to his side. Catharine pulled her horse aside one of the men, yanked his rifle from his hands and threw it aside.

"¡Estúpido!" she scolded. "¡Ayúdale!"

Annie was shocked to see the man cower, then dismount to help with Everline. His coat was already soaked in blood from his shoulder wound. The man removed a bandanna from around his neck, folded it and pressed it against the wound. Everline grimaced in pain. Annie removed her own bandanna and slipped it under Everline's arm and tied it as a tourniquet.

Both of the ranch hands gingerly eased Everline back into his saddle. After a few words from Catharine, Paco turned to Annie. "Señorita del Carmen will ride ahead so that help will be ready when we arrive." As he spoke the words, Catharine turned her mount back toward the ranch buildings and leaned forward in the saddle as the horse leapt forward and broke into a run.

The sun had already settled behind the hills and the once-white clouds were now a dusky gray. Light was fading fast as Glassford led Sean and Cheo toward the adobe walls of Los Cazaderos. Nicholson fidgeted in his saddle. What if Sean was right and these crazy Mexicans killed them all?

There was still plenty of animosity between the people of the two countries.

Then he had a second and equally disturbing thought. They might be paid the reward, but what were their chances of making it safely back to Texas? A lot of folks south of the border would know they had been paid off. He and Glassford could easily be targeted by bandits.

What seemed like a good idea for easy money back in Brownsville now appeared to be a death wish.

I'm a steamboat engineer, not a bounty hunter, thought Nicholson. *How did I ever get into this?*

His doubts and fears doubled as Los Cazaderos loomed ahead. Almost involuntarily, Nicholson let his horse lag behind. The gates to the estate opened. He counted five men at the gate. Suddenly, he wheeled his horse and spurred.

"Wally, what th–" Glassford yelled. He reached for his rifle, then relaxed his grip on the stock. "Now the reward is all mine," he said smugly.

Sean and Cheo saw Nicholson's retreat. Cheo's hands were almost free. "Dare I attempt it?" he asked himself. The men at the gate were armed. Cheo's hope faded. He might get away, but not Sean. No ... he would be turned over to Catharine's father.

Cheo knew he might well die, but before his death, he might be able to negotiate Sean's freedom. After all, his friend had no part in Cheo's fight with Carlos del Carmen. Señor del Carmen needed to hear this from Cheo. Cheo knew Glassford would lie about Sean to increase his reward.

Glassford spoke first. *"Tango el bandito, Cheo. ¿Donde es Señor del Carmen?"*

He could not understand the reply but allowed the men to surround his trio as they rode their horses through the gate. The only sound in the impending nightfall was the *clip-clop* of the horses' hoofs on the courtyard flagstones. Then the front hacienda door opened, and Carlos stepped forward.

Los Cazaderos

"I bring you the man who took your daughter," said Glassford.

"I see," answered Carlos, walking past Glassford. His eyes sought and rested on Cheo. He studied the tired, wounded bandit. Cheo sat erect, his shoulders squared and his eyes on Carlos.

"Why?" Carlos asked, his face a mass of stone.

"I heard you would pay a reward for –" began Glassford.

Carlos shot an angry glare at Glassford, who fell silent. Carlos fixed his stare on Cheo. "*¿Porqué, Cheo?*" he asked.

Cheo answered in Spanish, "Because, sir, your daughter and I are in love."

Carlos grabbed Cheo's arm and yanked him off his horse. Cheo fell on the flagstones and scrambled on wobbly legs to his feet. Cheo stood tall, looking into Carlos' eyes, ready for the blow. Out of the corner of his eye, Cheo could see Carlos' men raise their guns.

Cheo took a deep breath. "For Catharine, my love, I die gladly."

In a split second, he was pulled from the jaws of hell to the gates of heaven.

Carlos reached for Cheo and pulled the web of ropes from his hands. Then Carlos smiled and nodded. As Carlos embraced Cheo, his men aimed their guns at Glassford.

"Wha..." Glassford whined as he glanced about, his stomach knotted in fear, then he slumped in resignation and reached his hands to the sky.

Catharine and Annie stepped through the hacienda door. Both looking radiantly toward the love of her life.

"Annie!" cried Sean. He dismounted but remained tied to his horse. Annie rushed to him, smothering him with kisses, crying uncontrollably. She fumbled at his bonds.

"Señor Darragh, this man is your prisoner now," Carlos said, pointing to Glassford. Then he ordered his men to take Glassford's weapons and place the now pallid man in a cell.

River Run To Texas

As Carlos stepped back, Catharine rushed to embrace her lover. "*Mi corazón. Mi cielo*," she wept.

Walls of the great room glowed from the flicker of candles and oil lamps. Sean had bathed. Cheo was clean and bandaged. Paco was fast asleep in the servants' quarters. As a maid served wine, it was Annie who told how Everline saved them at the hotel, how Cyrus Fishborne took them to Matamoros, how Catharine stepped forward to lead them to the rancho and how Everline was wounded.

"He's upstairs, asleep, I hope," she said. "He's lost a lot of blood, but we believe he'll recover."

"This is a miracle," Sean said, still awestruck.

"The miracle is my daughter," Carlos corrected. "She did all these things, including the winning of my approval, while ..." He stopped in mid-sentence and turned to Catharine. "*Di les*," he commanded his daughter in a soft voice.

She put her arms around Cheo and announced, "*Estoy encinta.*"

As Cheo's swollen face registered shock, Carlos grinned and said, "Your beautiful bride is with child."

"Oh, Catharine!" cried Annie as she rushed to give her new friend a hug.

"Will you stay for the family church wedding?" Carlos asked Sean and Annie. "The priest will arrive in two days. It will be a grand feast. We'll celebrate for days."

"Of course," answered Sean. "Besides, we'll need to wait until Mr. Everline is well enough to travel back to Texas."

Annie snuggled under her husband's arm. Still unbelievably sore from her ride, she had but one request of her husband.

"Sean, please. Let's take the river home."

THE END

River Run To Texas

About the Author

George H. Chaffee
22041 Briarcliff Drive
Spicewood, TX 78669-2020
Phone: (512) 264-1507
E-mail: UncBillP@aol.com

Biography

George H. Chaffee of Spicewood, Texas, is a regular contributor to *GRIT* Magazine. His writing and photographs have appeared in *Country America*, *Tulsa* magazine, *The Kansas City Star* and many trade publications. This is his first novel.